C A LB

MY PILGRIM LOVE

MY PILGRIM LOVE

Veronica Black

Chivers Press · G.K. Hall & Co.
Bath, Avon, England   Thorndike, Maine USA

This Large Print edition is published by Chivers Press, England, and by G.K. Hall & Co., USA.

Published in 1997 in the U.K. by arrangement with Robert Hale Ltd.

Published in 1997 in the U.S. by arrangement with Robert Hale Ltd.

U.K. Hardcover ISBN 0–7451–6949–X (Chivers Large Print)
U.K. Softcover ISBN 0–7451–6961–9 (Camden Large Print)
U.S. Softcover ISBN 0–7838–1971–4 (Nightingale Collection Edition)

The text of this Large Print edition is unabridged.
Other aspects of the book may vary from the original edition.

Set in 16 pt. New Times Roman.

Printed in Great Britain on acid-free paper.

British Library Cataloguing in Publication Data available

Library of Congress Cataloging-in-Publication Data

Black, Veronica.
    My pilgrim love / by Veronica Black.
        p.   cm.
    ISBN 0–7838–1971–4 (lg. print : sc)
    1. Massachusetts—History—New Plymouth, 1620–1691—Fiction.
2. Pilgrims (New Plymouth colony)—Fiction.   3. Large type books.
I. Title.
[PR6052.L335M9   1997]
823′.914—dc20   96–35732

CHAPTER ONE

It was, Joy thought dismally, the worst fortune in the world that she should have been caught smiling in church. It had not been entirely her fault though Aunt Hepzibah could scarcely be expected to admit the fact. The trouble was that Aunt Hepzibah saw nothing comic about pastor Robinson whose scanty hair was combed meticulously across his high-domed pate and whose voice, in moments of excitement, squeaked exactly like the bats that swooped and wheeled about the spire of St Peter's church when dusk fell.

'Let us strive to be earthly angels,' Pastor Robinson had squealed, 'raising our hearts and voices to the Lord. Remember, my dear friends, that our Father in Heaven notices every sparrow that falls and counts every hair on the head of a man.'

It was at that point that Joy had been betrayed into a smile as the thought flashed across her mind that it wouldn't take the Lord very long to count the hairs on Pastor Robinson's head, and it was her misfortune that her aunt had been glancing sideways at the time.

Afterwards had come the lecture, delivered in that tone of gentle reproach of which Aunt Hepzibah was a mistress.

1

'A great girl of seventeen to forget the duty she owes to God in such a shocking manner! I could have sunk through the floor when I saw the ribald smile on your lips. Your dear parents would be turning in their graves were they to know of it.'

None of this was new. According to Aunt Hepzibah, Joy's father and mother, who had died of the plague when she was only a baby, spent most of their time in the afterlife whirling round and round in their graves. If she had looked suitably contrite then the matter would have been dropped but standing with downcast eyes and folded hands, Joy couldn't restrain a gurgle of mirth.

That was why she sat in her small bedchamber, forbidden to stir a step, while, in the parlour below, her aunt dispensed cordial and cakes to the various neighbours who had come to celebrate the death of the king. Festivities were rare in this small community and the more enjoyed on that account, and now she was cast out like a black sheep for what she couldn't help feeling was a very small fault. There was a mirror hanging on the wall, large enough to enable her to straighten the linen coif on her neatly braided hair but not so big that it would encourage vanity. From where she sat, on the low stool at the foot of the narrow bed, she could see her face, the nose upturned in a manner her aunt sighed over as impudent, the mouth too wide for beauty.

Only her eyes, set like sapphires beneath winged, dark brows, were truly lovely, holding as they did all her unexpressed dreams and hopes. For the rest her figure was too ripely curved, her skin peppered in the summer with freckles, her light brown hair straight as rain without the faintest tendency to curl. Usually these deficiencies were remedied by the dimple in her cheek that peeped out when she smiled and the glint of gold that tipped her long lashes, but she was, at that moment, too disappointed and too resentful to smile, and the face that stared back to her from the glass was plain.

The Sabbath was not a cheerful day at the best of times and it was rare for any kind of entertaining to go on in the small English community, but the death of King James was sufficient excuse to permit some relaxation of the rules. 'Except for me', Joy thought and jumped up impatiently to look out of the window. It was already dark and the flaring torches at the corners of the streets made pools of honey on the cobbles and were reflected in the waters of the canal. By day Leyden was a bustling and pretty town, but at night it took on an aura of mystery and romance. At least so it seemed from her window. Joy, who had never actually been out after dark, often spent hours staring out up the narrow street towards the canal, watching the occasional passer-by, making up tales of the exciting errands on

3

which they might be bound.

Tonight the torchlit streets looked more enticing than ever. She stared out for a moment longer, then whirled about, snatching her cloak from its hook on the back of the door. One short walk as far as Clock Alley and then she would come back and nobody would be any the wiser.

The narrow staircase led down into the kitchen out of which a side door opened into a small garden. Aunt Hepzibah grew herbs for the medicines she brewed in the little plot of land, one of her habits being never to trust an apothecary. From behind the closed door of the parlour came a murmuring of voices and the clink of a glass. Joy made a brief face at the door and went through the kitchen. The side door was unlatched as usual, the neighbourhood being law abiding and she passed into the dark, cool evening, pulling up her hood and opening the gate cautiously lest the click of the staple alert those within. The blinds, however, were drawn down over the parlour window and she was unobserved as she walked up the street to the distant gleam of water at the end.

During the day the quayside was lively with people. Merchants set up their stalls in the shadow of the warehouses that lined the wharf, lawyers argued cases while taking the air, children bowled hoops watched by anxious mothers who kept a wary eye on the distance between them and the water. Now it was deserted, only the hulls of the trading vessels rising darkly against the star-hung horizon. A chill breeze blew in from the harbour and the taste of salt was on her lips. She strolled along to where the bridge spanned the water and the beautiful stone houses of the richer merchants leaned together, their porches suffused with the glow of hanging lamps. A faint mist blurred the carved stonework and hung like dark lace about the tall masts of the ships.

Joy's steps slowed and stopped. She had not imagined that anything could be so lovely. It was a loveliness that caught at her heart and yet lacked the power to satisfy her. If only Peregrine were here to share it and not thousands of miles away in the Americas! She sighed deeply, bending her head to look down into the water whose dark surface sent back hundreds of dazzling reflections from the lights above.

Footsteps echoed hollowly down a nearby gangplank, and she was pulled back from the water's edge so abruptly that she almost fell, while a voice said sharply in Dutch,

'Don't be such a dumb fool! Nothing is worth the dying!'

'Dying!' she echoed him in English, struggling to free herself.

The lights had dazzled her and she could make out only a tall, broad figure looking down at her, but the tone of his voice had irritated her as much as his sudden appearance had startled her, and she rushed on heedless as to whether he could understand or not.

'Have the goodness to let me go at once, sir. At once! If you do not I will call the Watch!'

'You promise not to jump in?' he answered in English though his deep voice had the tinge of an attractive, unfamiliar accent.

'I've no intention of jumping in,' Joy said crossly. 'What on earth made you think I was?—you're English!'

'Irish,' he corrected, still keeping a firm grip on her arm as he steered her away from the glinting water. 'And maids who stand in the darkness on the quayside looking forlorn often end up in the water! It's a chilly night and I'd no wish to be catching my own death by having to jump in after and fish you out, though it's a pretty fish I'd be catching.'

They had reached one of the flaring torches and he paused, cupping her chin in his hand and tilting her face. She looked up into a reckless, smiling countenance, eyes the colour of the honey pools cast by the light, black hair flopping over a broad, tanned brow.

'I don't believe we've met, sir.' She felt suddenly uncertain under his bold and searching gaze.

'We've met now.' White teeth gleamed in the darkness of his face as he took a step back and swept her an elegant bow. 'Master Patrick O'Farrell, at your service, Mistress—?'

6

'Joy-in-the-Lord Jones,' Joy began and stopped. Her would-be rescuer had flung back his dark head and was laughing so infectiously that after a moment she felt her own lips twitch and a stifled giggle escaped her.

'Forgive me,' he said, still laughing. 'I was brought up to believe that it's very rude to laugh at a lady, but I never could get used to the names you people load on your children! Well, Joy-in-the-Lord Jones, what are you doing out here all alone if you're not planning to do away with yourself?'

'I was taking a stroll,' she said gathering together her dignity.

'Do your parents know that you are out alone?' he enquired.

'They died when I was a baby—and you're beginning to sound like Aunt Hepzibah,' she said.

'Don't you like your Aunt Hepzibah?' he asked.

'Most of the time,' she admitted, 'except when she makes me sit in my bedroom and miss all the celebration.'

'Ah, if it's celebration you're wanting!' He laughed again and seized her hand, pulling her with him away from the lights towards a house set back from the others.

'I can't go in there!' In alarm she pulled back. 'That's a bad house!'

'It's a tavern. A perfectly respectable tavern.'

'And taverns are bad houses. No decent

body would set foot in one.'

'Now *you're* beginning to sound like your Aunt Hepzibah!' he teased.

'Even if I do I still can't go in there,' she protested. 'Someone would be sure to see me and then I'd be in worse trouble than I am now.'

'Wait here for me then.' He glanced about and, seeing a bench set in the recess of a wall, drew her to sit down. 'One moment, that's all.'

He was gone, shrugging his cloak about his broad shoulders. From the open door of the tavern she could hear singing. The Dutch, unlike the members of the English colony, enjoyed their Sabbaths once the duty of church attendance had been fulfilled. Here in the shadows she was almost invisible and she sat back as far as possible, wrapping the cloak about herself.

He was back within the time he had specified, two brimming tankards in his hands.

'There! The ale's not as good as English ale, but it will do. Your good health, mistress!'

They clinked tankards and she sipped in the polite manner approved by Aunt Hepzibah.

'What are we celebrating by the way?' he enquired, sitting beside her and stretching his long legs before him.

'Haven't you heard?' She looked at him in surprise. 'The king is dead!'

'A week ago in England,' he nodded, 'but why celebrate it? What did Scotch Jamie ever

8

do to you?'

'He put some of the Brethren in prison and he fined our people when we didn't go to Anglican Services,' she said.

'You're a Puritan. I forgot.'

There was something in the way he said 'puritan' that irked her. Rather sharply she said.

'Separatists. We are not all Puritans. Some are Levellers and others Covenanters and others are—.'

'You're confusing me, darling!' he interrupted.

'And it's most improper of you to call me that!' she exclaimed. 'I'm not betrothed to you, you know.'

'Are you betrothed to anybody else?' he asked.

'Not exactly.' She shook her head, glad that the darkness hid her blushing. 'Are you?'

'Glory be to God but no!' He drained the rest of his ale in a couple of gulps and said, 'So you're glad King James is dead? Did he kill your parents?'

'They died of the plague when I was very small and Aunt Hepzibah took me to rear,' she explained. 'When I was about seven so many of our people were being put in prison that she decided to come over to Holland. We lived in Amsterdam at first and then, after a while, we moved here to Leyden.'

'How do you earn your living? As weavers?'

9

'A lot of us do, but Aunt Hepzibah and I make lace and she brews physic from the herbs she grows.'

'Drink up your ale,' Patrick said.

'It's stronger than Aunt Hepzibah gives me,' she admitted. 'She always says that strong drink addles the brains.'

'And you're already in trouble.' He took the tankard from her and put them both together on the ground. 'What exactly did you do?'

'I smiled in church,' she confessed.

'And that's a sin?' He tilted her face up again and smiled at her. 'Why were you named Joy-in-the-Lord then?'

'That's different. Joy doesn't mean levity in a holy place,' she said earnestly.

'You go to church a lot, I suppose?'

'Twice on the Sabbath and to Prayer Meetings on Tuesdays and Thursdays,' she nodded.

'With long sermons, I'll wager?'

'Longer than eternity,' Joy said fervently. 'Aunt Hepzibah likes nothing so much as a good sermon and she says that if I don't then I must have a natural leaning towards sin.'

'That's one of the most foolish statements I ever heard,' Patrick said.

'It's just her way. She's very good to me actually,' Joy said hastily, feeling a pang of conscience to be discussing her aunt behind her back.

'You should be married and have your own

household,' he remarked.

'One day I shall be, when Peregrine sends for me,' she confided.

'Who's Peregrine?'

'Peregrine Carver. He's a fine man—even Aunt Hepzibah thinks so. He and I were—not officially betrothed because I was too young but we had an understanding,' she confided.

'To marry?'

'Of course to marry. He wished to make his way in the world so he went to the Americas, to join the Mayflower colony in New England, and he'll send for me when he's made a home for me.'

'When did he leave?' Patrick asked.

'Three years since,' she began, and was interrupted by his long, low whistle.

'Three years! I'd call that a laggard lover!'

'You've no right to say that!' She crimsoned with indignation. 'Peregrine has a sense of responsibility, that's all. He works very hard and he has a high standard of morality.'

'And he's older than you are.'

'Seven years older,' she said.

'Only seven years!' he marvelled. 'From the way you talk of him I took it he was at least forty. I'll wager he's plain though, legs slightly bandy? A little squint in one of his eyes?'

'As a matter of fact he's very nice looking,' she said loftily.

'And he's not sent for you yet? Perhaps he never will.' His words were so close to her own

11

unspoken fears that a little shiver ran through her. She rose hastily, speaking with as much dignity as she could muster.

'He will send for me when he judges the time is ripe. It's late and I must be getting back before my aunt discovers that I slipped out.'

'I'll walk home with you.' He too had risen and stood, taller than she, vaguely disquieting so that involuntarily she took a pace backward and said quickly.

'That's very kind but there isn't any need.'

'You'll not deny me the chance of walking a pretty colleen home,' he said, tucking her hand through his arm in such a masterful manner that, short of kicking him on the shins, there was no way she could break free.

'Colleen?' she enquired.

'It's the Gaelic for a pretty maid,' he told her.

'You speak Gaelic, as well as Dutch and English?'

'And I can make shift to be understood in French and Spanish too,' he said. 'I've knocked about the world since I was taken by the press-gang when I was fourteen. Now I'm near thirty with my master's licence and my own boat.'

'You're a sea captain!'

'In a modest way. The *Bridget* was damaged in the spring gales and we put in at Delftshaven for repairs. So I'm land-locked for a month.'

'And where do you go then?' She had forgotten her irritation in her interest.

12

'To the Americas.' Under the torchlight he slanted a smile at her. 'The settlers need woollen cloth and books and I've a contract to deliver.'

'Have you been to the Americas before?' she asked eagerly.

'Three, four times. I'm my own master so I generally spend the summers there. The fishing's good and there's space for a man to stretch his soul.'

'Then you must know the New England settlements!' she exclaimed. 'Have you ever met a Master Peregrine Carver? He's tall with fair hair.'

'Not to my knowledge.'

'He sends back a letter to Aunt Hepzibah every six months or so to assure her of his continuing health, but it's a long time between letters,' she said wistfully.

'Doesn't he write to you?'

'We are not formally betrothed so it wouldn't be proper. Peregrine,' she explained earnestly, 'is a very proper man.'

'Is he indeed?'

They had reached the end of the street and, without warning, he swung her about to face him, pulling her so close that for an instant she lost her breath. In that instant his mouth pressed her own in the first kiss she had ever received. She had dreamed on occasion of the day when she and Peregrine would be betrothed and he would claim more than the

13

peck on the cheek he had so far taken, but this long and bruising caress was quite unlike anything she had imagined. For a moment, to her shame, she found herself clinging to him. Then she struggled free, wiping the back of her hand across her mouth, her eyes glinting as she spluttered.

'Sir, that was a dreadful thing to do!'

'Regard it as a message from Peregrine,' he advised.

'I will not! Peregrine would never—'

'Of course he's very proper, isn't he?' Patrick O'Farrell laughed. 'I am not in the least proper,' he said amiably, 'so if we are to be friends then you must take me as I am.'

'I don't intend to take you in any way!' Joy said stiffly. 'Goodnight to you, sir.'

Cheeks burning, her legs shaking with what she told herself was anger, she turned on her heel and marched down the street. She didn't look back but the soft echo of his laughter pursued her all the way to the garden gate.

CHAPTER TWO

'A letter from Peregrine? Oh, what does he say? Is he well?'

Joy's eyes shone with excitement as they rested on the parchment her aunt was reading.

'Do take events more calmly, my dear,' Aunt

14

Hepzibah protested, raising her eyes from the closely written sheet.

Her own hands, however, were far from steady and there was an unaccustomed tremor in her voice as she went on.

'Peregrine is in good health for which he thanks the Lord, and the settlement continues to flourish. Their harvest was good last autumn and enabled them to survive the winter. Goody Fairclough—you remember Goody Fairclough, don't you? She had the ague quite badly but is somewhat recovered.'

'Does he mention me?' Joy broke in, being not in the least interested in Goody Fairclough's ague.

'I am just coming to that.' Aunt Hepzibah settled her spectacles more firmly on her nose and, having run her finger with irritating slowness to the relevant paragraph, read aloud.

'Now that I have proved my virtue by the comforts I have amassed since my coming to this new land, it is my intention to offer honourable marriage to your niece, Mistress Joy-in-the-Lord. This cannot come as a great surprise to you for, though she was somewhat young when I left, I believe I had already indicated my affection and respect for her and that she returned those sentiments. I have built a fine wooden house and have a good parcel of land on which I raise corn and beans. I also have two cows and a large number of chickens.

15

Mistress Joy-in-the-Lord will not lack for comforts or female companionship, and Master Brewster continues to preach sermons that inspire us all. This being so and with your permission I request, therefore, that Mistress-Joy-in-the-Lord travel to join the settlement on the next boat.'

'He has asked for me!' Joy's voice rose as squeakily as Master Robinson's. 'He wants me to sail to the Americas and marry him!'

'There is no need to go into transports,' her aunt said but she smiled a little as she adjusted her coif. 'This is a very good letter, my dear. It reflects an estimable character.'

'Then you give your permission?' Joy clasped her hands together so tightly that the knuckles gleamed white and fixed her gaze beseechingly on the older woman.

'If you wish still to marry him,' Aunt Hepzibah said, 'then I will not prevent it.'

'And we can go to the Americas?' Joy said.

'My dear child, I have no intention of leaving Holland,' the other said. 'I shall soon be fifty and I doubt if I could endure a long sea voyage. My journey from London is still a most unpleasant memory!'

'Then I shall be travelling alone?' Joy's face fell slightly. The settlement was so far away and the prospect of going there seemed suddenly intimidating.

'You are seventeen now.' Aunt Hepzibah folded up the letter and clasped her own hands.

16

'It is time for you to make a life for yourself, my dear niece. I must confess there have been moments when I have been anxious about your future. Your dowry is only a modest one and no other man has offered for you. I am relieved, as well as happy, to give my consent.'

'And you will stay here?'

'I am scarcely likely to return to England with Charles Stuart succeeding his father on the throne,' her aunt said drily. 'He has even less sympathy for our people than King James had. No, I shall remain here in my little house. All my friends are here and my income is sufficient for me to live on. It will give me very great pleasure to think of you happily settled with a good husband.'

'How soon am I to leave?' Joy asked. The faint trepidation was fading and bubbles of excitement were rising in her. She was very fond of her aunt despite her strictness, but the prospect of leaving the confined existence she had always known thrilled her.

'This letter was brought by a packet boat that is going on to England, but there is a boat going out to the settlement in October, taking supplies for the winter.'

'October is six months off,' Joy said in dismay. 'Anything could happen by then!'

'I talked to the Harbourmaster this morning after I received the letter,' Aunt Hepzibah said. 'I fear that October is the earliest time you can hope to sail.'

Joy sighed. It was unreasonable of her to feel so discontented when for three years she hadn't even been certain if Peregrine would send for her at all, but now that the letter had come she wanted to leave as soon as possible so that she could be with him. The prospect of another long, slow summer was too much to endure, and the prim little parlour seemed more airless than usual.

'Will you excuse me for a while?' she asked. 'I'm so excited that I need to walk.'

'Don't be late for supper then. Good news ought not to affect one's punctuality,' her aunt said, never slow to point a moral.

'I promise.' On impulse Joy bent and kissed her aunt's thin cheek. 'Thank you for giving your consent. It isn't that I'm ungrateful—.'

'But you're anxious to be wed. I can understand that.' Aunt Hepzibah said. 'When I was a girl, only a year or two older than you are now, there was a young man. Ah well, the good Lord visited him with the sweating sickness and it was not to be, but I have not entirely forgotten my own hopes.'

There must have been a time when her aunt was young and hopeful, Joy realised, as she went out. Her young man had died and Aunt Hepzibah had been cheated of her opportunity to wed. Six months was a long time during which anything might happen. At this very moment, as she walked briskly towards the Rappenburg Quay, plague might have struck

18

the settlement and Peregrine already be dying. The thought made her heart stand still as she contemplated reaching the age of fifty with nothing but lace work to warm her old age.

She almost walked full tilt into Patrick O'Farrell before she realised he was holding her by the elbows and shaking her slightly as he exclaimed.

'Whenever I meet you, Mistress Joy-in-the-Lord Jones, you're headed for the canal! What mischief are you up to now?'

'No mischief, sir.' She wriggled loose and dropped a hasty curtsy. 'I wasn't looking where I was—oh, Master O'Farrell, I am so exceedingly glad to see you!'

'Are you now?' His eyes, creased against the sun's glare, twinkled down at her. They were not golden as she had imagined, but a clear, light brown fringed by lashes almost as long as her own, and in daylight his skin was tanned darkly save for a white scar that showed faintly along his stubborn jaw line. He was handsome, she supposed, in a strong, almost brutal way.

'I am so pleased to be the cause of your exceeding gladness,' he said, gently mocking.

Realising she was staring, Joy hastily dropped her gaze to his buckled shoes and said breathlessly.

'You are an answer to prayer, save that I have not yet prayed which only proves the great goodness of the Lord! You have not yet sailed.'

19

'In about ten days.'

'To the Americas. You are still going to the Americas, aren't you?'

'With woollen goods and books. I told you,' he reminded her. 'Did you reach your home that evening without being discovered?'

'Yes, quite safely. Will you take me with you to the Americas?' she asked eagerly.

'That I'll not!' he retorted. 'Do you know the penalty for aiding a maid to run away from her guardian?'

'I don't want to run away,' she said, clutching at his braided sleeve. 'I seek passage to the New England settlement as soon as possible and I have Aunt Hepzibah's consent.'

'Master Carver has written a letter!' He seized her hands, his eyes dancing.

'He has sent for me,' she said, her face glowing. 'He has asked for my hand in wedlock.'

'So you're betrothed?' He bent his head and, without warning, kissed the palm of her hands. Her fingers involuntarily curled as his lips brushed her flesh and she snatched her hands away with a nervous giggle.

'Master O'Farrell, there are people around! You will take away all my reputation!'

'The saints forbid!' His mouth twitched as he stepped obediently away. 'I was so overcome with delight at the news that you finally caught yourself a husband that I was unable to restrain my feelings.'

20

'You're laughing at me again,' she said reproachfully.

'A little. Now what's this about you wanting me to take you to the Americas?' he enquired.

'There isn't a ship sailing until October,' she explained. 'Not a regular ship that is. I had forgotten about your boat.'

'The *Bridget* is not a passenger vessel, but a small trading boat. We don't have any accommodation for women.'

'But I only take up a little space,' she said pleadingly.

'And a lone, unmarried female cannot travel alone with a crowd of sailors,' he went on. 'Even if your aunt were to allow it I could not. We would be six weeks at sea in cramped conditions and my crew is not a group of hymn-singing Separatists, but rough men with rougher manners.'

'Surely I could depend on your care,' she murmured. 'Or am I to believe that you cannot control your men?'

'I can control them,' he said shortly.

'Then will you—?' She gazed at him hopefully.

'How will you explain me to your aunt?' he wanted to know. 'The good lady is not going to take very kindly to the notion of you sailing off with a man you bumped into when you were roaming the town after dark!'

'You'll think of something!' Lighthearted now that her plea had been answered she

21

flashed him one of her heart-stopping smiles that lit her face with beauty, bobbed a curtsy and ran off.

No waiting until October! If good fortune stayed with her then by mid-July she could be arrived at the settlement and reunited with Peregrine. The prospect was a rosy one and she retraced her steps with a light heart, and ran up to her room with nothing more weighty on her mind than the need to sort out her possessions ready for the packing.

They were few and simple enough, Aunt Hepzibah being frugal by nature and in circumstances. A grey woollen gown, identical to the one she was wearing, a dress of dark blue silk to be kept for the Sabbath, three pairs of cuffs and collars, one pair edged with lace, two coifs, a shawl, stockings, underlinen and two nightgowns, together with two pairs of shoes composed her entire wardrobe. For the rest she had a brush and comb, a narrow box filled with ribbons, half a dozen books, a leather purse, a knife and spoon. It was not much with which to start a new life in a strange land, but at that moment it was sufficient that she was actually going.

The chest at the foot of the narrow bed where she had slept for the past ten years held the two articles she had been stitching ever since Peregrine's departure. She lifted the lid now and drew them out. The quilt which would cover her bridal bed was made of padded squares of material culled from old scraps left over from the sewing the Ladies Circle worked at during their twice-weekly meetings. Here was a piece of Goody White's bridal gown and a bit left over from a cloak that Mistress Wheelwright had made for her granddaughter. In taking it with her she would be taking memories of all the people with whom she had grown up in this little colony of English exiles.

Beneath the quilt lay the gown she had been making for her wedding day. It was the most splendid dress she had ever owned, its skirts of deep saffron, its low neckline trimmed with a deep collar of creamy lace. There was a coif of matching lace and she turned it about over her hand, smoothing it with a gentle finger.

From below voices sounded. She raised her head, listening, colour rushing into her face as she recognised the deeper voice. Folding the gown and the quilt she laid them back in the chest, closed the lid and rose. A hasty glance in the mirror reassured her that her hair was neatly braided and her coif straight.

She went downstairs slowly, tapping on the parlour door as she entered. Aunt Hepzibah, looking slightly flustered, was the first to speak.

'Joy, the most amazing coincidence!' she exclaimed. 'No, it must be the will of the Lord! This gentleman here is actually sailing to the settlement in about ten days.'

'Captain Patrick O'Farrell, mistress, at your

service.'

He made the small room look even smaller as he rose from the chair where he had been sitting and bowed over her hand.

'Captain.' She dropped a curtsy and tried to match his gravity.

'The captain's ship is at Delftshaven undergoing repairs,' Aunt Hepzibah said, waving him back to the chair. 'He is taking supplies out to our people there, and he has been kind enough to offer you passage.'

'I met with the Harbour Master,' Patrick O'Farrell said smoothly, 'and he told me a young lady wished to travel out to be married. I was glad to offer help, though I fear my ship is a modest one and the accommodation on it somewhat limited, but Polly will be good company for your niece. Polly is going out to New England too and will be pleased to have another female with her.'

'Joy, bring in some cordial,' her aunt began, but Patrick interrupted, raising his hand.

'I beg you, no,' he said. 'I make it a habit never to drink cordial until after sunset. Indeed I seldom take any even then.'

'A cup of milk perhaps?' Aunt Hepzibah suggested.

'Nothing, truly, though I thank you kindly. I have business to transact in Leyden,' he said.

'Do you sail from Delftshaven, captain?' Joy found sufficient voice to enquire.

'The Lord permitting,' he answered so

solemnly that she bit back a giggle.

'Amen to that,' Aunt Hepzibah said. 'I see you are a God-fearing man, captain, but I've not seen you at church.'

'I've not been here more than a few days,' he said. 'I must confess that my profession makes it difficult for me to attend Divine Worship as frequently as I would wish.'

'One can understand that.' Aunt Hepzibah had unbent completely and beamed upon her visitor. 'Your profession is a most dangerous one, sir. I often pray for those at the mercy of the wind and the waves.'

'At this time of the year the ocean is like a millpond,' Patrick said. 'Indeed, that was one reason why I was so bold as to offer my services to Mistress Joy-in-the-Lord. In October there are frequently storms that might easily drive vessels off course, and you would experience great anxiety on your niece's behalf.'

'That is most thoughtful of you. Is it not thoughtful of the captain, Joy, to consider such a thing?' Aunt Hepzibah appealed.

'Amazingly thoughtful,' Joy agreed.

'Of what religious persuasion are you, captain? We are Covenanters ourselves but I have acquaintances who are Levellers.'

It seemed to Joy that he hesitated for the barest fraction of a second before he spread his hands and said, smilingly.

'Are we not all Separatists, mistress?'

'Indeed we are and may the Lord keep us

25

inviolate in our separateness,' she responded.

'And I must leave.' He rose and bowed over her hand. 'I will send a boat for Mistress Joy-in-the-Lord to bear her and her luggage to the *Bridget*. That is the name of the ship, after my dear mother.'

'A pleasant compliment,' she said.

'Mistress, if you were to sail in her,' he returned, 'I'm sure the ship would be renamed before she reached the first port of call!'

'You will turn my head with compliments!' she exclaimed, looking far from displeased. 'Joy, you may walk with Captain O'Farrell to the end of the street and point out St Peter's to him. If your business brings you here again, sir, I hope you will find time to worship there.'

'I hope so too, mistress.' He bowed again and stood aside politely to allow Joy to pass through into the narrow hallway.

In the street she could restrain herself no longer, her tone of indignation mixed with amusement as she exclaimed.

'Not take cordial before sunset indeed, when I saw you with my own eyes quaffing ale just as fast as you could!'

'Ale is not cordial,' he answered blandly. 'And do keep your voice down, darling! Do you want to ruin my reputation?'

'I'm not your—' She flushed, biting her lip.

'That you're not!' he agreed amiably. ''Tis just a bad habit of mine to be calling every woman darling. You're another man's now that Master Peregrine Carver has taken it into his head to send for you. And shouldn't you be thanking me for contriving to take you on my ship when you feared that you'd have to wait until October?'

'Oh, I do thank you, sir,' she said earnestly. 'I am most exceedingly obliged for your help—but it was very wrong of you to cozen my aunt so shamelessly!'

'Would you have me lurch through your door smelling of rum and singing a sea shanty?' he grinned.

'No, of course not! But all that about Polly—as if you had another female on board!'

'Polly is very much of a female,' he assured her. 'She would be most insulted if you failed to believe in her existence. For the rest it would be no true kindness to your poor aunt to have her thinking she was sending you off in charge of a rogue. Her mind will be at ease now and you can pack with a light heart. Can you be ready in ten days?'

'I could be ready in ten minutes,' she informed him.

'Could you now?' He turned and looked down at her. ''Tis to be hoped Master Carver appreciates your eagerness to be with him.'

'He is a most admirable man,' she began.

'He has good taste in women anyway,' Patrick said.

Something in his expression made her back a step, saying hastily. 'There is St Peter's, sir. My

27

aunt wished me to point out to you.'

'Very pretty.' His eyes were still on her face and his mouth twitched at some private amusement. Even in sober doublet and hose he had a quality of recklessness that attracted her against her will. Breathlessly she said.

'In ten days then. I am most obliged,' and fled back down the street.

CHAPTER THREE

At the last moment it was harder than she had anticipated to leave the home she had shared with her aunt for as long as she could remember. She had not realised how fond of her Aunt Hepzibah was beneath her strict, unyielding manner, nor how difficult it would be to part company with the people with whom she had grown up. Most of them gave her small gifts that they had made themselves—a book of rag leaves on which each girl had embroidered her name, a pincushion fashioned in the shape of an apple, a length of fine lace.

'We had to hasten to get them finished in time,' Prudence Goodright explained, 'but a bride ought to set out for her wedding with gifts from her friends. Oh, Joy, I think you're very brave to travel so far to be married!'

'No braver than those who sailed out in the beginning,' Joy said. 'They didn't know what

28

they would find when they landed. Now the settlement is flourishing and Peregrine Carver will be waiting for me.'

She spoke with a glad optimism, aware of the admiring envy in the other girl's voice. Prudence had been betrothed for nearly five years and her man had still not named the day. Now she said wistfully.

'Will you wear your bridal gown? The one you have been stitching?'

'Of course. It's ready, all but the hem.'

'Mine has been ready for ages,' Prudence said.

'How happy you will be when you wear it then,' Bethel Lowrie murmured.

'John will set the day as soon as the roof on his dwelling is finished.' Prudence bit her lip and flushed slightly.

'She would be better to sail with you to the settlement,' Bethel whispered to Joy. 'John Foster will find something else to do when the roof of his house is on and thus delay the wedding yet again.'

Joy frowned her into silence but her own heart was full of relief. If Peregrine had not written she, like Prudence, might be waiting with a bridal gown already yellowing in its layers of lavender-scented paper.

Her possessions were now stowed away in a capacious leather bag and Aunt Hepzibah had given her a prayer book and a wooden box filled with ointments and tisanes she had

29

compounded herself.

'Health for the soul and for the body, my dear niece,' she said briskly. 'Look after them both now and you will live to be a good age.'

'I will come back and visit you long before then,' Joy assured her.

'You will have a new life to lead,' her aunt said firmly, 'and it is of no use to begin it by looking back at your old one. Master Carver is an honest, industrious man and you are a most fortunate girl. Make up your mind to be a good, faithful wife and don't make plans to waste your husband's money in spinning back and forth across the ocean.'

There were several such lectures before the actual day of departure. Joy wondered a trifle ruefully if Aunt Hepzibah had decided to give her a lifetime's moralising all at once. As it was she listened as attentively as she could and, when her aunt was bidding her a final farewell, received the ultimate accolade.

'Had your dear parents been spared,' she said, 'they would, I believe, have just cause to be a little proud.'

'Dear aunt!' Joy embraced her with real affection and stepped down into the narrow barge that would ferry her to the harbour at Delftshaven. Her aunt, blowing her nose into a large handkerchief, stepped back among the little group of well-wishers on the quayside and waved. Joy, blinking back sudden tears, raised her own arm, craning her neck for as long as possible as the figures diminished and a curve hid them finally from view.

The journey to Delftshaven was only a short one. Aunt Hepzibah had almost decided to accompany her on the first stage of her journey but had changed her mind.

'There is nothing sadder than saying goodbye and watching a ship grow smaller and smaller, my dear. We will part at Leyden.'

Joy had been to Delftshaven twice before on marketing expeditions and been excited and confused by the bustling crowds who thronged the port. This time she was too intent on trying to pick out the *Bridget* from among the other tall-masted vessels to notice the swarming people haggling for fish and fruit as the trading boats emptied their holds.

She heard Patrick O'Farrell's voice above the splashing of the oars and looked up to see him standing on the deck. He had discarded his sober garb and his doublet of dark leather was laced over a shirt of brilliant scarlet that made his hair look blacker than ever.

'So Johannes brought you safely? I swore I'd have his hide if he did not! Grip the ladder, mistress, and climb up.' The ship was not large, but it seemed to loom over her as she gripped the sides of the iron ladder and cautiously climbed up, kicking aside her hampering skirts and trying not to glance down at the water.

'There's a good maid!' Patrick leaned over the low rail of the sloping deck and lifted her aboard, setting her down before him and holding her as she stumbled. 'Steady! it will take you time to get your sea legs! Your aunt didn't come with you then?'

'Did you feel that she might?' Joy challenged.

'She would never have made it up the ladder,' he said gravely. 'Come, I'll show you your cabin. There are only three on the *Bridget* and, as one is mine and the other my chief mate's, you'll have to share yours with Polly.'

He took her arm, a proceeding she deemed slightly unnecessary, and escorted her down a sloping companionway into a long, low, covered area with benches at the sides. There were several pigtailed men seated on them, and their chatter ceased as she was led past them.

'Your crew?' she asked.

'My crew,' he nodded. 'I've warned them to wash out their mouths and keep their eyes to themselves now there's a lady aboard, so it's likely they'll stay dumb until the end of the voyage! Mind your head. There's not much space here.'

Obediently she ducked her head, negotiated a short flight of wooden steps, and ended up in a tiny cabin lit by a flickering lamp. As she entered an ear-splitting shriek from the shadowy corner made her jump violently and clutch at Patrick's sleeve.

'That's Polly greeting you,' he said, amused, and leaned towards the corner, whistling deep in his throat.

There was a fluttering of wings and a large green bird curved its talons over his shoulder, rubbing its beak against his cheek.

'Polly is a parrot!' she exclaimed.

'And a most respectable female, as I assured your aunt,' he told her. 'She's big for her sex. Female parrots are usually smaller but this one is healthy and hearty and fathoms deep in love with me as you can tell!'

'Will she come to me?' Joy asked.

'Hold out your arm and whistle—can you whistle?'

'Too well,' she said ruefully, remembering past scoldings.

'Whistle soft then, one short and two long. It's Polly's call signal and she always obeys it.'

Joy did as she was instructed and started slightly as, with a whirring of wings, the large bird settled herself on her wrist, curving her talons with surprising gentleness about Joy's sleeve and cocking her head to one side, as she peered into her face.

'She likes you,' Patrick said, but his comment was drowned by a sudden, raucous exclamation from the bird.

'Hell and damnation, how are you, m'darling?'

'She talks!' Joy cried.

'And she's picked up some terrible language,' he said gravely, his lips twitching. 'You'll have to excuse her for she's not a

33

church-going bird.'

'In which I suspect she resembles her master.' Joy shook her arm slightly and Polly flew back to her perch and clung there, glinting green in the shadowy corner.

'Not at all. I go to Mass when I can.'

'To Mass? Then you're a Papist!' Her tone was one of horror as tales of rack and rope whispered in the firelight swarmed into her mind.

'Did you ever meet an Irishman who wasn't?' he asked.

'I never met an Irishman. Oh, how could you be such a thing?' she enquired indignantly. 'Have you never heard of the cruelties practised by the Inquisition? No wonder you didn't wish Aunt Hepzibah to know! She would never have dreamed of allowing me to set sail with a Papist!'

'I said I was a Separatist, not one of the Anglican Communion and that's true. For the rest of my beliefs are my own and I make no apology for them.' A hint of steel had crept into his voice and was gone as he said, 'The *Bridget's* still at anchor and I can have you rowed back to Leyden if you give the word.'

'And wait until October?' She shook her head decidedly. 'I will sail now, sir.'

'Master Carver is fortunate,' he said dryly. 'You take great risks for his sake.'

'As he would for mine,' she said sharply.

'Here's Johannes with your baggage.' He

stepped aside as the thick-set Dutchman ducked into the cabin and set down her trunk. 'I've to see about the raising of the anchor now before we miss the turn of the tide. You can come up on deck if you promise to keep out of the way.'

'I promise.' Abandoning the argument that had sprung up between them she followed him meekly.

She had watched before the loading and unloading of barges and small boats, but it was a different matter to be actually aboard as the men swarmed up the rigging and the sails were released from their folds to swell as the breeze caught them and the deck, responding to the tugging of the tide, rose and fell beneath her feet. Ropes were being coiled and made fast and above her a tall thin individual in a striped doublet was bawling out a long string of what were to Joy incomprehensible orders. She wondered what veering one's lifters and hauling one's braces to the yard could possibly mean. The pigtailed men, sleeves rolled up above tattooed forearms, muscles straining beneath leather doublets, obviously understood clearly however. The deck lurched as the wind seized the vessel and then, briskly and smoothly, the *Bridget* began to move away from the wooden wharf.

The sea was not the blue of the distant horizon but slapped grey-green against the timbers. Joy leaned over to watch it, oily

35

beneath but foamed with white like the lace she and Aunt Hepzibah had made. If her aunt knew that she was setting out to cross an ocean with a Papist and a parrot! For all her misgivings Joy could not prevent herself from laughing out loud and one of the sailors, sweating as he wound up rope nearby, sent her an amused glance.

The tall, thin man had descended from his eyrie and was approaching her. Close to she saw that his face was seamed like old leather and his hair was greying.

'Daniel Patterson, mistress, first mate. The captain's compliments, ma'am, and there's food below if you've a mind to join him.' He bowed as he spoke but there was no real friendliness in his eyes. Joy had the distinct impression that Daniel Patterson was of the opinion that a lone female aboard ship was a very bad idea. She would have liked to stay on deck as they headed into the channel on the south-westerly course that had been set, but she was beginning to feel hungry and so nodded an assent and turned to follow the first mate below. He left her at the door of a cabin adjacent to her own, raising his voice to announce sullenly.

'Lady's here, Captain Patrick.'

'Come and eat.' Patrick opened the door and motioned her into a low, darkly panelled chamber with portholes on one side, a large table on which maps and papers were strewn

36

and a curtained recess to which her eyes involuntarily strayed.

'My sleeping quarters.' Patrick, whose own eyes evidently missed nothing, waved his hand towards a smaller table flanked by a couple of high-backed chairs. 'You can explore later if you wish, but, for now, you'd do well to get some food inside you. If you're going to feel queasy you'll feel worse on an empty stomach.'

'I don't intend to feel queasy,' Joy said, accepting the chair with dignity.

'Eat anyway. It'll be about six weeks before we taste fresh food again,' he invited.

'It seems a long time to be out of the sight of land,' she said, beginning to eat the roast lamb he was piling on her plate. 'This is delicious!'

'I've an excellent cook. He can make even weevilled bread taste palatable.' He filled his own plate, topped up two wine glasses, and sat down opposite her.

'Your first mate doesn't like me,' she said abruptly.

'Daniel doesn't like any woman unless she's past fifty and old-looking at that!' he informed her. 'He had his fingers badly burned once and he blames the entire sex for it. He knows more about the sea than most men have forgotten, however, so I put up with his ill-considered opinions.'

'You don't share them then?' She could not resist slanting him a sideways look that held teasing in its depths.

37

'I love all women, darling,' he said blandly, 'but there's not the one who's caught me yet. When she does I'll trade in my ship for a nice little manor house back on Irish soil and settle down to be the envy of my neighbours!'

'So you're not wedded to the sea?'

'I learned long ago never to set my heart too strongly upon anything,' he said lightly. 'Even the *Bridget*, much as I adore her, is no more in the end but a shell of wood, to be sunk or broken up in the scrapyard when her usefulness is ended.'

Instinct told her that behind his lack of concern lay a tale, of a love lost or betrayed, but he was not going to confide it. With an air of changing the subject he said. 'So you've been to sea before! Do you remember it?'

'Vaguely. I was only seven.'

'And that was ten years since and a shorter distance. We sail along the English coast and round Land's End, so you'll see the shores of your birthplace at least.'

'And then it's the ocean.' Her blue eyes shone darkly. 'Is it truly like a millpond at this time of year?'

'Let's hope so. With a freshening wind we can make the tip of Cape Cod within six weeks.'

'And without it?'

'Then we'll likely drift for a couple of years,' he said. 'Do you think you'll enjoy that?'

'I want to reach the settlement,' she said

earnestly.

'To marry Master Carver.' He nodded, one side of his mobile mouth lifting wryly. 'Drink your wine. At least while you've got your mouth full I don't have to listen to a catalogue of Peregrine's perfections.'

'That,' said Joy, swallowing wine too fast and spluttering, 'was exceedingly rude.'

'So it was!' He gave her an amiable infuriating grin. 'We'll make a bargain then. You won't tell me more than three times a day that you're looking forward to reaching the settlement and I will refrain from what comes into my mind to do every time I see you.'

'What's that?' she asked and could have kicked herself for her stupidity as he half-rose, leaned across the table, and kissed her full on her startled mouth.

'Sir, I told you before!' She drew back hastily, almost upsetting her wine.

'Mistress, I cannot resist teasing you a little—you are so deliciously prim,' he said solemnly.

'But you must not! I am promised.'

'To Master Carver! You will have to remind me of the fact from time to time after all lest I forgot myself again. You could say "Hepzibah" every time I look as if I am about to embrace you,' he said.

'Master O'Farrell, you're a fool!' she exclaimed, unable to restrain her laughter.

'Call me Patrick,' he said.

'As if you were my brother? I never had a brother.'

'And I will call you Joy—in a sisterly fashion, of course!' His brown eyes were creased with amusement. 'Come, finish your meal and I'll show you the ship. There are parts where you cannot go—the cargo in the hold pitches and rolls in a rough sea and might crush you, and you'll have to content yourself with a view of the crow's nest from below!'

'I'd like to climb the rigging,' she said impulsively.

'The Lord forbid!' His voice was fervent. 'Some of the crew are not too happy about having a woman aboard in the first place. If they saw you swarming up the rigging on your way to the crow's nest half of them would mutiny!'

'And the other half?'

'Oh, they'd be following you up to the crow's nest,' he declared, cocking an impudent eyebrow at her.

She reached hurriedly for an apple and sunk her teeth in it, aware that her cheeks were as red as the fruit. He was, she decided, a coarse-grained man for all his charm and he took so much pleasure in embarrassing her that he had obviously been very carelessly brought up.

'Does Master Carver know that you have a dimple in your cheek?' he asked abruptly.

'I don't know.' The question was so unexpected that she stared at him blankly.

40

'I suppose that he has a soul above such matters,' Patrick said consideringly. 'I suppose he hasn't even noticed that your cheekbones are sprinkled with freckles that look just like specks of nutmeg or that your ankles are the trimmest I ever spotted.'

'It is three years since we met,' she countered. 'He probably remembers me as I was when I was fourteen.'

'And now you are much older.' His eyes were unexpectedly kind. 'And him? I take it that you remember him clearly?'

'Of course I do!' There was a trace of defiance in her voice. 'Peregrine is tall and fair-haired and his eyes are—are blue.'

'Like a young god, I suppose? You're sure his eyes are blue?'

'I'm sure, and I thought you didn't wish me to talk about him,' she said.

'True, but mention of him curbs my natural impulses,' he grinned. 'Come and see the rest of the *Bridget*. She's a beauty, fit to grace the widest sea.'

He held out his hand and, after an instant's hesitation, she put her own hand into it, feeling the slightly rough warmth of his palm as his fingers clasped her own. Peregrine had blue eyes. She reminded herself sternly of the fact as they left the cabin together.

CHAPTER FOUR

She had not imagined that a ship was so complex nor the sailing of one so dependent upon the skill of the men aboard. With increasing respect she listened and watched as Patrick explained the two compasses, one to plot the course of the vessel, the other to calculate the distance they had travelled in a given time.

'We set the watch by the compass too. Every four hours. When we're in known waters, or within sight of land, it's an easy matter to calculate direction and distance but, when we're out in the open sea, then we need to find our latitude and for that we use quadrant and astrolabe. They give us the patterns of the heavens and the lead and line give us the depth of the sea.'

He was quite a different person when he was explaining his craft, Joy thought. His expression was intent and absorbed and he paid her the compliment of talking to her as if she were an intelligent person and not merely a girl. Standing by him she was conscious of her own small, curved self next to his broad shoulders and length of thigh and leg. His black hair, ruffled by the wind, blew in elflocks across his temples and she had to restrain an urge to reach up and smooth it down.

'How long is the line?' Conscious that she was staring she hastily framed a question.

'Two hundred fathoms. It's marked with knots at every ten fathoms,' he explained. 'When the line reaches bottom, bits of sand and shell cling to the lead, so we can measure how far below the seabed is.'

Involuntarily she glanced over the side. The sun was setting and its red glow turned the water into wine. Far, far below was the bottom with its sand and shells—

'And the bleached white bones of drowned men,' Patrick said, picking up and completing her thought. 'Wrecks too, stripped clean by the fishes, the barnacles clinging to their hulls and the tattered sails waving gently in the dark water.'

'Don't!' she said shuddering.

'Do you not like a little touch of terror to spice your days?' he enquired. 'Most people shiver and protest but the old tales fascinate them.'

'They will fascinate me too, when I'm on dry land again,' she said firmly. 'Tell me about the cargo you carry.'

'Woollen goods mainly, for the winter months,' he told her. 'Winter on the eastern coast can be vicious and nobody has any sheep there yet. And books, Bibles and Prayer books and collections of sermons—you Separatists are a godly lot! Hornbooks too, so that the children can learn how to read. They're setting up a school, I think.'

'And I shall be part of it all,' she said softly. 'Living in a new land, being happy and busy.'

'You've planned it all out?' he said.

'I shall have the house to keep and a garden to plant and sewing to do,' she said.

'And that will content you?'

'It contents most girls,' she said.

'I had reckoned you as more of an adventurer.' He leaned against the rails and stared down at her. 'Wasn't it yourself who was itching to climb up the rigging?'

Joy tilted her head to look at the billowing sails and said, frowning. 'I think I gave up that ambition,' she said primly.

'I'm delighted to hear it,' He spoke as solemnly as she, then let out a shout of laughter, putting his arm about her shoulders and turning her about as he pointed.

'What is it?' She narrowed her eyes and saw, leaping out of the water and curving in a glittering arc of rainbow spray something that shone silver in the dying rays of the sun.

'Dolphins,' Patrick said. 'They're playing leapfrog in the water. There are some men who swear that dolphins have a language of their own, a real language.'

'Why are they leapfrogging?' she asked with interest.

The arm about her shoulders tightened and there was a note of surprise in his voice.

'They don't need a reason,' he said. 'They

44

play because they play. Didn't you ever do that?'

'Aunt Hepzibah says that play is the devil's occupation,' Joy said. 'It must be directed to good ends if it's to be allowed at all. That's why little girls are given dolls, to teach them how to be good mothers when the time comes for them to have children.'

She stopped abruptly, astonishment striking her dumb for with quick, impatient movements he was tugging off her coif and pulling loose the ribbons that confined her hair.

'Look at the dolphins!' he commanded. 'See how the sun makes patterns on their backs and breathe! Breathe in the salt and the wind! Doesn't it make you want to play for no other reason than you are alive?'

She was not certain exactly what she wanted to do at the moment. The deck swayed beneath her feet and over her head the great sails strained against the tarred ropes. Ahead of her she could see the dolphins describing perfect arcs in showers of glittering spray and at her back, as he held her secure against the motion of the ship, Patrick's voice was warm breath in her ear. A ripple shivered up her spine and she felt slightly dizzy though she had drunk only a little of the wine.

Unsteadily she said, 'You confuse me. You put thoughts into my head I never had before.'

'Oh, the thoughts were there,' he assured

45

her, 'but I helped you to recognise them. That's all!'

'Thank you—for showing me the dolphins.' She drew away, conscious that the rippling within her had spread and intensified until it seemed that her nerves were tipped with liquid fire. Patrick was aware of it too. She could sense amusement in his voice as he said.

'I'm not about to claim credit for the dolphins or for the sunset, my pretty, but I flatter myself I made you feel them. Beauty's to be felt, not merely seen.' He had wound a long strand of her hair about his fingers and now he tugged at it gently as if to emphasise his point.

'You can't touch the sunset,' she said, gasping slightly because it was suddenly hard to breathe.

'I was not looking at the sunset,' he said softly, and his eyes were flecked with tiny points of gold. He was so close, so close she could see the faint white scar along his jawline, the shadow of his lashes above his cheekbones. He was too close, she thought in panic, and took a step backwards, saying in a high voice that didn't sound like her own.

'I think I will go to my cabin now. I believe I'm starting to feel a bit sick.'

'Liar! You're a born sailor,' he said amiably, but he had slackened his grasp on her hair. She rummaged hastily for her coif, but he held it just out of reach, his eyes twinkling.

'You have soft, pretty hair. Why hide it

under a linen cap?'

''Tis the custom, as you well know. St Paul instructed all females to cover their hair.'

'St Paul had some very foolish ideas,' he said, but yielded the coif. She thrust back her hair and tied the cap ribbons firmly under her chin.

'Now you are armoured again,' Patrick said, raising an eyebrow at her. The uneasy feeling that he could practically read her thoughts swept over her. He was, she guessed, a man experienced in the ways of women. She had never met anyone quite like him before. In Leyden the small community of English Separatists had kept themselves very much to themselves, the men either being respectably married or working industriously towards the day when they could claim their sweethearts as wives. Their Dutch neighbours had accepted them but the two groups seldom mixed, and Joy's knowledge of men was perforce limited.

'I thank you again,' she said, blushing.

'Goodnight to you then, mistress.'

Either taking pity on her embarrassment or tiring of his sport, he bowed politely and stood aside to allow her to pass along the deck. There were several of the crew about, some coiling ropes, others swabbing down the rails with wet sponges. Evidently warned to behave, they nodded pleasantly as she went by, but she guessed that once she and Patrick were out of sight there would be some ribald muttering.

'The lamp will burn all night,' he said, pointing to it as it swayed on its hook in the cabin. 'It's quite safe. With so much wood and tar about fire is one hazard we guard against most strictly. You won't be thrown out of your bed if the ship rolls either. There is a side on it that bolts into place and keeps you as snug as the cargo. Shall I take Polly?'

At the sound of her name the bird squawked loudly.

'If you take her than I will have told a lie to Aunt Hepzibah,' Joy said solemnly. 'She believes me to be chaperoned by another female, remember?'

'Are you always so scrupulous in your honesty?' Patrick asked.

'I try to be,' she said simply.

He shook his head in half-pretended disbelief and went out.

Alone, Joy sat down on the narrow bunk and looked about her. The cabin was much smaller than the one Patrick had given her the meal in but it was not too cramped. Everything was either ridged on top or bolted to the floor. Even Polly's perch was skewered down, she noticed, and wondered if the crew of a ship expected rough weather as a matter of course.

'Hot water, mistress?'

A grimy-faced lad, who looked as if he could have done with the application of a little soap and water himself, hovered in the doorway, a steaming jug in his hand.

'Thank you, Master—?'

'They call me Mick,' the boy volunteered.

'Is that your name?' she asked, watching him wedge the jug in a hole in the centre of the table bolted to the panels.

'Don't rightly know,' Mick said cheerfully. 'I was known as Greaser on the docks on account of my job was to grease the guns before they hoisted 'em broadsides. Massive big guns they was! Big men-o-war, only I never got to go on them! Then Captain Patrick—he picked me up between jobs, asked me if I'd like to go to sea proper. 'Course I said I would and then he said real sailors ought to have a real name. So he picked Mick.'

'Why Mick?'

'Because I had a dog once of that name,' Patrick said, stepping back into the cabin which immediately shrank in size. 'Get this Mick started on his life story and he'll keep you a captive for the rest of *your* life! Get back to your post, boy. You're due to stand watch.'

'Can I have a chew of tobacco?' Mick enquired.

'You cannot—it'll stunt your growth.' Patrick cuffed him lightly through the door and turned back smilingly to Joy. 'He's a good lad, but he's not really fitted for a sea-faring life. The boy lacks roots. That's what he's always lacked and he clings to me because he sees me as a kind of security. I've a mind to buy him an apprenticeship out in the New World.'

'In the settlement?' Joy looked at him in surprise.

'Why not? They need settlers, don't they? Or are you surprised to learn I've got a social conscience?' he retorted.

'I am beginning to be surprised at nothing.' She sat down on the bunk and stared up at him in exasperated amusement. 'You seem like six different people in one person. The captain of a fine ship, an Irishman, a Papist, a—.' She hesitated, blushing scarlet, clutching her lower lip in her teeth.

'Do go on,' he invited. 'It's fascinating, quite a list.'

'Did you want anything in particular?' she asked.

'A dangerous question, my pretty colleen,' he said.

'If you're going to tease—!' she began indignantly.

'I came to tell you that you'd do well to stay in your cabin until the decks have been sluiced down in the morning,' he said. 'I'll have some breakfast sent to you.'

'Thank you very much. That's very kind of you,' she said meekly.

'On the contrary, I am seldom kind,' he told her, 'unless there is some advantage to be gained. You'd do well to remember that, my pretty Joy-in-the-Lord!'

He had ducked out again before she could answer him, closing the door. From her perch

Polly observed tartly, 'Well damn my eyes!'

'Your language is quite shocking,' Joy said severely as she began to take off her dress.

It was fortunate that the Separatists disapproved of the elaborate, wide-skirted fashions that were in vogue, else she would have needed the services of a maid. As it was her simple gown with its wide linen collar was easy to manage alone. She stood for a moment in her shift, conscious of the play of the lamplight over her bare shoulders and arms, turning her skin to creamy rose. Below her breasts were round and full curving into a small waist. She ran her hands lightly down over her rounded hips and shivered without quite knowing why.

'What a sight to see!' Polly exclaimed, so appropriately that Joy wondered if the bird had some understanding of what it said.

She reached to unfasten her trunk and take out the long-sleeved, high-necked nightgown, slipping it over her head before she removed her shift.

'It's not wise to gaze too long upon the naked flesh even when it is our own,' Aunt Hepzibah had said, neatly paraphrasing Elder Robinson.

Flesh covered one's bones and was to be kept clean. There were sins of the flesh to be avoided at all costs. The trouble was, Joy decided as she splashed her hands and face with the water, that nobody was ever very

51

specific as to what the sins of the flesh were. As she brushed her long hair she remembered how Patrick had wound a strand of it over his fingers and the queer shiver ran through her again.

She got hastily into the bunk and lay for a while, watching the lamp move to and fro, listening to the creaking of the timbers. Somewhere above her head a bell clanged and someone shouted an order. In the corner Polly had put her head under her wing. Beyond it all she could hear the wind gusting and the slap-slap of water against the bows. In a moment she would have to get out of bed to say her prayers. People who lay abed framing petitions to the Lord did not, in Aunt Hepzibah's estimation, deserve to be heard. Even as Joy was thinking that her eyelids were fluttering down, her breath becoming deeper and more even—and then there was only the ship rocking her into dreamless slumber.

She woke, bewildered for an instant not to find herself in her room at home, and then was wide awake. She had no idea what time it could be but, from the sounds of activity outside the cabin, guessed that it was morning. She had scarcely dressed and tied the linen coif over her hair when there was a thunderous knock on the door and Mick came in, bearing a tray on which bacon and bread and a tankard of ale were placed.

''Morning, mistress. Captain Patrick says he

hopes you slept hearty and to step careful when you come on deck. Sun generally dries it out but there's the devil of a fog coming up,' he said cheerfully.

'Thank you. I slept very well.' She returned his grin.

'Damn my eyes!' Polly shrieked, emerging from slumber.

'That bird,' said Mick, 'needs converting!'

'She's not very ladylike,' Joy agreed. 'Do you know what time it is?'

'Past six, mistress. Halfway through the Watch. Eat up your breakfast before it gets cold. There's nothing worse than cold bacon on a foggy morning.'

He sounded positively maternal. Joy stifled a grin and sat down meekly to eat her meal, while Mick took up the jug of cold water and bustled out importantly. He was a nice lad, she thought, and it was no wonder Patrick had taken an interest in him.

'Mick, would you like to have a real job?' she asked. 'An apprenticeship—'

'You've been talking to Captain Patrick!' he accused, swinging about with the jug in his hand. 'He's forever on about me settling to the land.'

'Don't you like the land?' she enquired.

'I like where the captain is,' Mick said firmly and marched out.

Joy finished her breakfast, straightened her bed, folding the nightgown beneath the pillow, and stepped out, holding on to the rail as she made her way up to the covered area. Three of the crew were finishing what was evidently a hasty meal. The others were on deck. She could hear voices and footsteps distorted by the blanket of white mist that had settled over the ship. She returned the men's greeting and went cautiously out into the mist, holding on to the guard rail.

The ship lurched suddenly and she let out a gasping cry as her feet slithered over the wet deck. She was brought up short by a coil of rope to which she clung, its rough texture scraping her palms. An instant later and she was gripped firmly in two arms while, above her, Patrick's irate voice sounded.

'Holy Mother, will you never stop running to the water's edge every chance you get? Didn't I tell you to stay in your cabin until the decks were dry?'

'I wanted to see where we were,' she protested.

'You and the rest of the crew!' Even in the gloom she could see the flash of his white teeth. 'We're creeping down the Channel, darling, hoping to God we don't drift near any rocks! These summer fogs can lift as suddenly as they come down or linger for days.'

'Then we'll not see the coastline of England?' she said, disappointed.

'If we do, in this fog, you can take it that we're shipwrecked,' he said. 'Now go on back

54

to your cabin and keep out of mischief!'

'You talk to me as if I were a child,' she began resentfully.

'To remind myself that you're not.' He held her more closely for a moment and then shook her gently and said, 'Hepzibah!'

'I beg your pardon?' she said, puzzled.

'Hepzibah! That was the word you were supposed to use when I seemed to be in danger of embracing you.'

'Oh.' She hesitated for a moment, then said in a small voice. 'Hepzibah then.'

For a moment she thought he was going to embrace her anyway and her lips parted as she swayed towards him, but he gave her another shake and a push in the direction of the cabin and went off again into the mist.

CHAPTER FIVE

Joy, balancing on the rail and looking out across the wide expanse of blue water, had never felt more at peace with herself. Her face was lightly tanned by the long hours of sunshine that they had enjoyed in the weeks since the *Bridget* had entered the Atlantic and her long hair blew out behind her in the wind. All round, as far as the eye could see, were the waters stretching to the horizon where a band of darker azure marked the separation of sea and sky.

After more than a month at sea she had begun to feel as if all her life had been spent above a creaking, swaying deck, or in a tiny cabin where a green parrot sat swearing in the corner. She was rather proud of the fact that she had not felt queasy once though the quality of the food had sharply declined. Even the excellent cook found it difficult to make tasty meals out of dried scraps of meat, and bread so hard that it had to be soaked in water before it could be chewed. Water was now strictly rationed and all the men save Patrick sported beards. He still found water enough in which to shave every other day and his doublet, as stained with seawater as any of the crew's covered a brilliant shirt which he changed every week. Joy suspected that he was more of a dandy than he would admit and the thought that he had a weakness pleased her.

Certainly he had shown no signs of any other weakness in the time since she had embarked. His manner towards her remained a mixture of affection and mockery, and he had not touched her since that first fogbound morning. Joy told herself that she was very glad he was behaving so respectfully and then jumped slightly as he strode along the narrow deck towards her. It seemed that she often was thinking of him at the moment he appeared.

'Isn't it a perfect day?' She greeted him smilingly but, to her surprise, he frowned, shading his eyes with his hand as he looked up into the sky.

'There's a storm due,' he said.

'On such a beautiful day! Surely not!'

'The wind has a warning in it,' he said. 'It's beginning to drop when it ought to be freshening, and those lead-coloured clouds over there are the heralds of a storm.'

'You sound terribly gloomy,' she complained.

'I know this ocean,' he told her, 'it's as fickle as a woman, sweet smiling one moment, then sullen and brooding, and finally boiling over with fury. No reason for such changes of mood.'

'You don't think much of women, do you?' she challenged.

'I told you that I love them all,' he said lightly, but the bleakness was back in his eyes and it was not caused by fears about the weather.

'But you don't respect them,' she persisted.

'Only when they're old and past temptation,' he said.

'That's what Parson Robinson always used to say,' she said resentfully. 'Females are weak creatures to be lectured and sheltered and guarded against.'

'Perhaps he spoke from experience,' Patrick said.

'As you do?' She looked up into his face, trying to fathom the expression on it but he

57

turned aside and peered out across the ocean again.

'No dolphins today,' he said. 'When a storm is brewing they seek more sheltered places.'

'I was thinking of the first ship that came to the Settlement,' she confided. 'Five years ago—I was only a child but I could feel the excitement in my bones. We stood on the quayside to wave them off and we didn't even know if we would ever see any of them again.'

'The *Mayflower* made it.' His grim expression relaxed somewhat. 'There's something in the human spirit that won't admit defeat.'

'The wind has dropped.' She glanced up at the limp sails, aware of an imperceptible ache at her temples.

'And there are the storm clouds rolling up. You'd do best to go to your cabin if you fear rough weather.'

'How can I tell,' she asked reasonably, 'until I've been in it?'

'Don't fall over the side then.' He gave her a slightly irritated grin and was gone from her side.

The activity on board had increased. The men were lashing down anything movable, trimming the already lifeless sails. Usually they whistled or chanted as they worked, but today they were almost as grim as their captain. One of them, coiling a length of rope and making it fast, jerked his head at the darkening sky and spoke sourly.

'Big 'un's coming, mistress! Better get below soon.'

She compromised by moving back into the covered area where she could still see the panorama of waves and sky. The sunshine no longer glittered on the water and the blue sky was a purplish-bronze, heavy-brooding shade that seemed to press down around the ship. The slight headache that always presaged thunder nagged at her temples again and she drew a deep breath, listening for that first rumble that would release the fury of the elements.

It came with a blinding flash of blue that clawed open the sky and lit the surrounding water with an unearthly glow. Large drops of rain spattered on the deck and a wind came up out of nowhere billowing the sails. The sky was dark now, as if night had descended in the middle of the afternoon, and the sea was furrowed, each furrow higher than the last. An instant the *Bridget* hung, poised between two troughs, and then, with a shrieking of wind that tore through the rigging, her prow dipped down as the waves crashed over the deck.

Joy clung to the wooden struts that held fast the roof of the covered place as the ship righted herself only to plunge down again into a towering wall of water that curled foam white at the edges. The rain was a blinding curtain, lashing the deck, and the wind had risen to screaming pitch.

She heard, above the wind, the cry to batten down the hatches and, fearful of being thrust down into the cabin, bent her body into the wind, hanging on to whatever her fingers could find as she inched her way along the heaving deck towards the railed stairway that led up to the wheelhouse. Dimly through the driving rain she could see Patrick hunched over the tiller, the wind blowing his hair across his face.

She gained the steps, her own hair plastered to her head, her skirt sodden. A flash of lightning haloed her and she skidded on the wet timbers, crying out as she scrabbled for a foothold, her hands locked about the stair-rail. A wave, higher than any she had yet seen, menaced her, breaking over her head with a ferocity that robbed her of breath. Salt-water filled her nostrils and blurred her eyes, and then she was free of the water as it receded and being hauled up the remaining steps into the wheelhouse.

Patrick might have looked grim before but now he looked positively murderous as he thrust her against an upright post, holding her in a grip of steel with one hand while, with the other, he sought to steady the wheel.

'Why the hell didn't you go below?' he shouted.

'Because I didn't want to be battened down like the cargo!' she retorted gaspingly.

'You could have been washed overboard, you little fool!' he interrupted. 'Here, Daniel!

Take the wheel and hold her steady!'

The First Mate, tall and thin in a striped and soaking jersey, took the wheel silently, darting a glare at Joy that spoke volumes.

'I don't fear the storm!' she said quickly, raising her voice above the howling of the wind. 'I do fear being shut away below!'

He wasted no time in arguing, but seized a rope and whipped it about her, binding her fast to the beam.

'Now if the ship goes you go too!' he mocked in her ear, and turned to take the wheel again, motioning Daniel away.

More water poured over them and the wind blotted out all other sounds. Risking a glance upwards she saw lightning zigzagging about the mast and then the ship dived down, timbers shuddering as she descended and rose up on the crest of the following wave. A feeling of exhilaration flooded Joy. She was beyond fear, looking down at her own small self secured to the post as the little ship battled through waves higher than itself. She never knew exactly how long she clung there, struggling for each breath, deafened by the crashing of the thunder. It might have been an hour or much longer. She had lost all sense of time, even all her sense of terror. A few feet away Patrick wrestled with the tiller, his feet in their high boots planted well apart, his hands gripping the wheel with an authority born of skill and experience. He was part of the ship, part of the storm, and she knew that she would always hold the memory of him in her eyes.

Incredibly the sky was lightening, the thunder and the wind dying into a grumble, the waves lessening as the vessel righted herself. They had outrun the storm, she realised, and ahead of them the horizon glowed in delicate tints of rose and gold.

'Any damage?' Patrick yielded the tiller to Daniel and called down to the men scurrying below.

'Couple of leaks portside, captain!' someone called back.

'Get them caulked. Any damage to the mast?'

'Not that we can see, but the cargo's listing a mite!'

'Get it secured and then let out the spritsail! Well, Joy-in-the-Lord Jones, are you still enjoying the storm?'

He had turned to speak to her, his expression suddenly teasing. Rain water still blew into his face and thickened his lashes.

'It was wonderful,' she said huskily, and began suddenly to shiver violently.

'You're soaked,' he said, his brows rushing together in their familiar frown.

'To the skin,' she agreed weakly, and looked down at herself. Her gown was so wet that it clung to her breasts, outlining their curves and the gentler slope of hips and thighs.

'I'll see to Mistress Joy. Keep her steady and check the compass, Daniel.' Patrick spoke briskly, bending to untie the confining rope about her waist.

Freed, she felt her knees buckle under her and instinctively clutched at him.

'Up you come!' With no ceremony he hoisted her over his broad shoulder and swung himself to the deck. The timbers glistened with salt and the breeze was sharp and tingling on her face. Overhead men clung like flies to the rigging as they hoisted more sail.

In the cabin Polly sat morosely on her perch, greeting them with a disapproving squawk.

'Poor old girl! She hates rough weather,' Patrick commented.

He had dumped Joy on the bunk as casually as if she were a sack of flour and now, bending over her, began to strip off her garments expertly, unhooking her bodice and rolling down her stockings in the efficient manner of one who had undressed a woman before.

'Sir, I beg you!' she began protestingly, but her fingers were too stiff to resist him or to manage the task alone, and her teeth were chattering.

'Keep still unless you want to catch your death of cold,' he ordered, reaching for a blanket and wrapping her in it. 'It would be a great pity if you 'scaped drowning only to sneeze yourself into an early grave!'

He had snatched up a towel and was winding it about her dripping hair. Beneath it her eyes focused on him in sudden awareness that she was stark naked under the concealing blanket, that the shivering had become a trembling sweetness that flamed along her nerves, that his brown eyes were searching her face with the same awareness.

Then his mouth was on hers, his hands pressing her against him, pressing her so close that their heartbeats were mingled and the blanket no more than a trifling barrier. Somehow her arms were about his neck and she was tasting salt from his lips.

'Damn it to hell!' He broke away, pulling down her arms, holding them in a bruising grip while anger flared in his face. 'I swore I'd never fall victim again!'

'Victim?'

'Never mind! You're a lovely, lovely creature, and I must have been insane to let you persuade me into bringing you out here!' he said violently.

'To reach the Settlement,' she said, blinking back unexpected tears. 'To reach—.'

'Master Peregrine Carver. I know! The golden-haired, blue-eyed lad who will make you into a contented, respectable, Godfearing wife.'

'You don't have to shout,' she interrupted.

'Not shout? You sit there in that foolish blanket with your eyes like blue stars and expect me to make polite conversation!' He jerked her to her feet, holding her shoulders, his eyes raking the contours of her body as the towel slipped lower. There was a hunger in his face that both alarmed and thrilled her but she no longer felt the cold.

'Wake up, Mistress Joy.' His voice was lower but still intense. 'This game you play is a dangerous one for I am no boy to be teased and cozened. You cannot cut your teeth on my heart!'

'Let me go!' She spoke without heat, her eyes on his temple where a pulse beat fast.

'You say that and your eyes still beckon me,' he said bitterly. 'I could take you here and now and there would be nothing you could do to prevent me.'

The thought flashed into her mind that there was nothing she wished to do to prevent him. She swayed towards him, her eyes half-closed, warmth shivering through her limbs. His mouth was hard against her own and the wet leather of his doublet rasped her breasts as the blanket fell in swathes about her feet.

'If I take you,' he said thickly, 'you will hate yourself and hate me too, because this cannot be the beginning of anything, not while you are still on your way to marry another man.'

She had forgotten Peregrine completely. It was even impossible to recall his face. She stood within the circle of another man's arms, her face still damp from the sea-spray, and the features of the man who had sent for her blurred into a mist.

'I am promised.' She dragged the words up

65

out of herself. 'You must help me to remember that I am promised.'

'By all the saints, but you try a man too far!' he said and pushed her from him so roughly that she almost fell. He thrust the blanket at her, his face so savage that she could have mistaken his expression for hatred.

Wrapping herself in it she sat down shakily on the edge of the bunk, and he turned and went out, swinging the door shut behind him. In the corner Polly said loudly.

'Well, damn my eyes!'

'Oh, be quiet, you stupid bird!' Joy pulled the blanket higher and shook her hair loose, not caring that the wet strands were down her neck. She didn't much care, she decided miserably, if she caught her death of cold. They would bury her at sea, she supposed, and there would be no more need for her to worry about anything.

With a fluttering of wings Polly flew to her shoulder and nestled there, peering up into her face with a look of such curiosity that despite her misery Joy couldn't help smiling.

'You're a fool, Polly,' she said and shooed the parrot to the end of the bunk where it balanced on the rail, watching with apparent interest as she towelled her hair. She would have liked to curl up in bed until the voyage was over and never set eyes on Captain Patrick O'Farrell again, but that was the coward's way.

66

She took out her Sunday dress and wriggled into it. Her skin was still faintly damp and there was the flavour of salt on her lips. She put on a dry pair of shoes and picked up the wet garments tossed over the floor.

The breeze would start to dry them at least if she could find a line to hang them on. Salt water stained clothes but there was not enough fresh water left to be wasted on laundry. It was safer to keep her mind firmly fixed on practical problems. Then she might banish the tormenting vision of what might have been.

'I'll see to them, Mistress Joy,' Mick said, coming up and taking the pile of sopping clothes from her. 'That was a grand storm, wasn't it?'

'Grand,' she said bleakly, and went cautiously across the deck to grip the rail. The sea was a mass of sparkling waves barred by a faint Jacob's ladder. It blurred her eyes, or so she told herself, trying to ignore the drops that splashed down her cheeks.

'Joy.' Her name, spoken by his voice, sounded unfamiliar and beautiful.

She went on staring at the emerging Jacob's ladder until her eyes ached, determined not to turn her head but conscious in every nerve that he stood near enough for her to touch.

'I'll not apologise for being a man,' he said, 'and you must feel no shame in being a woman. Perhaps you're truly innocent. Lord knows some women still must be, but I'll not steal any female from another man. I have a life of my own, plans of my own, and you have no place in them.'

'It will be better when we land,' she said chokingly. 'This ship is—is small.'

'And we are trapped upon it for the next two or three weeks, longer if we run into another storm.'

'Do you think we will?'

'It's always possible. Didn't I tell you the Atlantic was as fickle as a woman?'

His tone was light and bitter again. She wanted to cry out that it was not always so, that she was as steadfast as a rock, but shame kept her mute. She had behaved like a trollop with a man she scarcely knew and not given a thought to the steadfast lover who waited patiently at the other side of the world.

'Don't take everything to heart so,' he said in a kinder voice. 'We must remember to say "Hepzibah" more often, that's all.'

His hand touched her shoulder briefly and she gripped the rail more tightly, saying in a small, miserable voice as he moved away.

'Hepzibah! Hepzibah!'

The word had lost all its meaning and the Jacob's ladder hurt her eyes more than ever.

CHAPTER SIX

They had sighted land very early that morning and, a strong breeze behind them, were making for it. Patrick had called her up on deck to point out the low-lying spit of brownish-green that rose on the horizon.

'I am always a mite sorry to see that,' he told her. 'It's the end of the voyage and it means that the world will soon be pressing in again. Being at sea suspends one in a kind of limbo.'

Joy knew exactly what he meant. The past weeks had been something plucked out of time. She felt as if she could hold them between her hands and look at them as if they were quite separate from her real life.

'You'll be glad to see your friends again,' he continued, glancing at her.

'I've messages and letters for nearly everybody,' she told him. 'Will there be anyone to meet us?'

'Depend on it, the instant they see the sails they'll be sending a welcoming party down to the beach,' he assured her.

She wondered if Peregrine would be there to greet her and then remembered that he had no idea she was aboard. Still, he might be among those who came to receive the expected supplies. The thought didn't give her as much pleasure as she imagined it would.

69

Since the storm Patrick had kept her at arms' length, treating her with an impersonal courtesy that he might have displayed to a woman twice her age, but she was more conscious of him than ever. His long legs marched into her thoughts as regularly as they bestrode the narrow decks, and his voice sounded in her ears, now issuing some command to his crew, now telling her that the ocean was as fickle as a woman.

'Is that Cape Cod?' She indicated the spit of shore.

'We round the tip and anchor in the bay,' he explained. 'I leave a skeleton crew aboard and we go ashore in the long boat.'

'We?'

'I'll take Mick ashore and see if I can get him that apprenticeship I mentioned. Daniel will stay on board and act in my stead. Most of the cargo can be towed to the beach.'

'Mick wants to stay at sea,' Joy said.

'Mick doesn't know any better. When I ran across him he was wandering half-starved round the docks, sleeping rough and taking what work he could get,' Patrick said. 'At least he ought to have the chance to find out what a decent life on land is all about.'

'If I were a boy I would sail with you,' she said.

'You're the wrong shape,' he said briefly and, for a moment, their eyes met and locked in a long look that told her he had forgotten

70

nothing of what had passed between them.

'Patrick.' She spoke his name on a long breath, but he shook his head and spoke quickly as if to avert some danger.

'I've no doubt they'll be pleased to see that you've come before your expected time. No anxieties about your sailing during the winter months.'

'No indeed!' she said brightly, taking his cue. 'I suppose there are many more dangers in the winter.'

'There's danger at all times,' he said, and she knew he was not referring to the storms.

After a moment he said, too casually, 'I will stay a week or two myself.'

'In the settlement?' her heart seemed to skip.

'The good people there are too godly for my tastes,' he said, sending her heart plummeting again. 'I'll take the boat down the creek to the Indian village.'

'Savages?' Her eyes were wide.

'Algonquin sagamores,' Patrick said, looking amused. 'Massasoit is their Chief and a good friend to the settlers. If it hadn't been for the help of him and his people there wouldn't be any Settlement at all.'

'Oh.' She thought ruefully that she clearly still had a great deal to learn and, hard on the heels of that thought, came the wish that Patrick could be the one to teach her.

'You've brought supplies before, of course,' she said somewhat hastily. 'It seems odd you

71

never met Master Carver.'

'Not so odd. There were nearly three hundred people the last time I visited and when I've done my trading I go inland to stay in the Algonquin village, so I don't know many of the settlers personally save for Brewster and Standish.'

'I knew Master Brewster in Leyden. He was a very good man, pleasant in his manners.'

'He still is. Standish has a temper to match his red hair, but he's shrewd and experienced. They've treated the sagamores fairly and kept the treaty they made with them, as far as I know. It's a couple of years since I came out.'

'And much might have happened since then.' Her voice was small.

'Not much, I daresay,' he said, careless and comforting. 'It's, what? four months since Master Carver penned his letter?'

'About that. Aunt Hepzibah didn't mention a date.'

'Surely he wrote privately to you at the same time!' Patrick exclaimed.

'I told you before that it would not have been proper since we were not formally betrothed,' she said.

'And Master Peregrine is a very proper man.'

'Yes, he is!' she said defiantly, while the thought crept unbidden into her mind that Peregrine would not have compromised either of them if he had sent her one short note to say he hoped she would come.

'Peregrine's uncle was the first governor here,' she said defensively. 'He must behave correctly in order to give example.'

'As you say.' His lip curled slightly and she had the uncomfortable impression that her defence of Peregrine had been less than effective.

Excusing herself she went down to the cabin. Another hour, less if the breeze held strong, and they would be dropping anchor, lowering the narrow boat in which they would land at the edge of the shallow water. The voyage of nearly seven weeks would be over. She ought to be feeling thankful and excited, but she could only think of the wind that had howled through the rigging and of Patrick's strong hands on the tiller, the devil-may-care grin with which he had met the fury of the storm, the taste of salt on his mouth.

There was a footfall beyond the door and she swung about, eagerness in her face, but it was only Mick, looking as gloomy as she suddenly felt.

'Captain Patrick says if you're all packed I'm to take your baggage up,' he said.

'I'm nearly ready.' She reached for her cloak and tied it about her shoulders. 'What's the matter? You don't seem very happy at the prospect of landing!'

'Captain Patrick's said that I have to get a job on shore, settle down to land life,' he said

73

miserably.

'He's thinking of your own good,' she said.

'I wish he'd not trouble then. Nobody went thinking of my good before and I reckon it's too late now,' the boy said obstinately.

'Wouldn't you like to settle in the New World?' she asked. 'You could have land of your own one day. There's plenty of land there I should think.'

'Enough to make a body dizzy,' he agreed dismally. 'Why, mistress, I'd not know what to do with all that land!'

'If you like,' she said on impulse, 'I will ask Master Carver if he can take on an apprentice.'

'Live with you, mistress?' He gave her a sudden knowing look. 'I reckon Captain Patrick would be keeping in touch then from time to time.'

He had put into words the thought she was reluctant to admit even to herself. In her haste to leave Leyden she had neglected to take into account the fact that she would be cooped up for several weeks with a dangerously attractive man who was none too scrupulous in his dealings with women.

'What do you know about the Captain?' she asked abruptly.

'He's a fine man, mistress,' the boy said. 'I never met a better one!'

'I wondered if you knew anything of his life,' she said, despising herself for asking.

'He's from Ireland, but his people are dead.'

Mick, who for all his youth seemed to have a middle-aged liking for gossip, brightened up. 'He was pressed into the Fleet, but he sailed on expeditions against Spain and made sufficient prize money to buy himself out and get his own ship. He don't talk much about his life, come to think of it.'

'And he's a Papist.' In sudden misgiving she said, 'If you're a Papist too then it might not be such a good idea to join the Settlement.'

'Oh, I'm not anything in particular,' Mick assured her. 'We never go to church anyway. Captain Patrick says that God's everywhere so you don't need to seek him in a house with a roof on top and an altar at one end.'

'You had better keep such opinions to yourself,' she warned him severely, 'if you get an apprenticeship in the Settlement.'

He shrugged to indicate his indifference to what people in the Settlement might think of his opinions, and bent to pick up her trunk.

'We'll be landing soon, mistress,' he said. 'You'll be meeting your young man then.'

It was as if he reminded her that the dream was over and real life approached as the shoreline drew closer. She paused to take a last look round the tiny cabin, regretting not what had taken place but what had not happened. Mick had gone out, weighed down by the trunk, and as she stood there Polly flew to her shoulder and clung there, cocking her head inquisitively.

75

'Goodbye, Polly. I'm going to miss you,' she said over a lump in her throat.

'No need for goodbyes,' Patrick informed her, putting his head in at the cabin door. 'Polly's going with you, if you'll accept her.'

'But she's your bird,' Joy protested.

'Been with me for five years,' he nodded, 'but I don't believe in getting too attached to anyone. She likes you.'

'How can you tell?' she asked.

'She's not bitten you yet, has she?' He gave her the quick grin that lighted up his tanned face. 'Anyway, I'd like to give you a wedding present.'

'That's very kind of you,' she said, and felt as if in giving her the bird as a gift he had widened the distance between them deliberately, making it crystal clear that he had never had the faintest intention of becoming seriously involved.

'I told you before,' he said, 'that I am only kind when I need something in return. Polly's becoming a nuisance. I'd be grateful if you'd give her a good home.'

'I told Mick I'd ask Peregrine if he could take him as an apprentice,' she said.

'Polly's one matter,' he said curtly, 'and Mick's another. I'll settle Mick where I think he'll be happy.'

'Peregrine and I would treat him very well,' she began indignantly.

'I know that you would, but I've my doubts

about Master Carver,' he said.

'You don't even know him,' she interrupted.

'I've learned a little. He's the kind of man who keeps a maid waiting for three years, and then writes to her aunt to tell her he's decided to wed the girl. If he's so careless about her feelings then he's not likely to be too concerned about a waif and stray like Mick.'

'That's not fair,' she said. 'You're being unfair!'

'I'm not fair,' he said, banishing Polly to her perch with a flick of his fingers. 'I'm not fair and I'm not kind. Remember those two things about me. It will make your life much easier when you're married to Master Carver.'

His hands were on her shoulders and they stood close together in the dim cabin. She looked up at him, the trembling beginning deep inside her as her eyes drank in his face, feature by feature, from the unruly black hair that tumbled over his brow to the mobile mouth above the square chin.

'Go and marry your respectable Peregrine Carver,' he said. 'I'm a hard man, mistress, a man with a grudge, and there's no place in my life for you or anyone like you.'

He bent, kissed her so savagely that she feared he had drawn blood, and went out. There was nothing more to be said, she realised. Beneath his lightly teasing manner he was pure steel, haunted and driven by something she couldn't understand. Drawing a deep breath she whistled Polly to her shoulder and followed him up on deck.

The land was much closer now. She could see trees beyond the shore and dots of black moving along the water's edge. There were people waiting to greet the ship. She stood by the rail, the breeze blowing her cloak back from her shoulders like wings, while the anchor was dropped and the longboat lowered to the sparkling water. One or two of the crew approached to shake her hand and wish her Godspeed.

'Reckon you brought us luck, mistress,' one of them said, 'for we'd a good crossing, but now that you're leaving we don't have to guard our language so close!'

She laughed, wished him good fortune in return, and then with the sullen Daniel guiding her down the ladder was helped into the boat, with Polly fluttering down the rungs to join her.

'The harbour's too shallow to come close,' Patrick said, swinging himself down to sit beside her.

He had on the scarlet shirt and a new velvet doublet of mulberry, and she had a moment's keen pleasure as she looked at him. With his black hair and tanned skin he could wear brilliant colours that would have swamped another man. She wanted to tell him that he reminded her of some bright seabird but he was speaking briskly, as if they were strangers just

78

met, and his eyes avoided her.

The people on shore were waving as they crowded down to the water's edge. At her side, still not looking at her, Patrick said, quick and low, 'If I have disturbed or offended you, mistress, then I ask pardon. It's a long time since I had much to do with a respectable female. My life has no place for them. I wish you happy in your marriage. I sincerely wish you happy.'

His hand rested on his knee. She had only to move her own hand to touch him. With an effort of will she curled her fingers tightly and said.

'I thank you, sir, and wish you all fortune.' There was no time for more. Patrick had risen and was splashing through the shallows and the boat was being dragged clear of the water.

Joy recognised Master Brewster at once. He was shaking hands with Patrick and his hearty voice reached her clearly.

'Captain O'Farrell, this is a most pleasant surprise! We had not expected you so soon. The Lord gave you safe passage and safe landing then? May He be praised for that!'

'We had one storm but it caused little damage, and no loss of life or cargo,' Patrick said.

'May God be thanked! But you have brought more than cargo!' Brewster's eyes had travelled to the boat and rested on her.

'Do you recall Mistress Joy-in-the-Lord

79

Jones?' Patrick stepped to the boat and helped her to climb out on to the pebble strewn sand.

'Indeed I do.' Master Brewster was shaking hands with her cordially. 'My own daughter, Fear, is a year or two older. We did not think to see you until winter!'

'Mistress Jones accepted passage with me so that she could arrive the sooner,' Patrick said.

'Peregrine will be delighted,' Master Brewster said warmly. 'He is in the town—yes, we call it a town now though I fear 'tis a slight exaggeration! I trust your aunt is well? Mistress Hepzibah was one of our most revered citizens.'

'Very well, sir, but she declares she is past the age for travelling!'

'There will be some who will have to change their minds if Holland and Spain make treaty,' Brewster said. 'However, until that time, we will send greetings to those who remain in the Old Land. You showed a true courage in coming alone so great a distance.'

'Thank you, sir, but it was comfortable, save for the storm,' she responded. 'Captain Patrick has been most—most attentive.'

'I'm pleased to hear you say so.' Brewster dropped her hand and turned again to Patrick. 'You'll eat with us tonight, sir? You and your crew?'

'I'll accept on my own behalf,' Patrick said promptly. 'On young Mick's too. I'm hoping to settle him in your community, if you'll take him. For the rest, some fresh food sent out to the *Bridget* would be welcome to my men.'

'And the cargo? We'll need to talk prices.'

'We can do that before we eat,' Patrick assured him.

'We'll make for the town then, mistress. Can you make shift to walk a mile?'

'I think so,' Joy said.

In truth the firm ground that only shifted a little as her foot moved on the sand felt most peculiar. She would have liked to clutch at Patrick, but he had strode ahead with some of the other men, and it was Master Brewster who offered her his arm.

'I am grown accustomed to a heaving deck,' she apologised.

'Many of us suffered from the same discomfort when we first landed,' he told her. 'Were you greatly sick?'

'I was not sick at all,' she said proudly.

'The Lord gave you fair weather and a strong stomach,' Brewster said. 'There are many whom you will remember. Others, alas, died during our first harsh winter, but there have been others born since to fill the spaces. A Settlement needs younglings.'

They were moving up from the sloping beach and the trees that straggled from clumps of grass, their trunks wreathed with sea-holly. The air still tasted of salt and the sunlight glinted on the cutlass at Patrick's side, drawing her eyes like a magnet even while she inclined her head politely to Master Brewster's flow of gentle-sounding chatter.

CHAPTER SEVEN

The settlement looked like a fort or a prison, Joy thought, as they emerged from the trees into a cleared space. Ahead of them reared a wooden pallisade topped with sharp-pointed spikes. As they drew nearer she saw that the wide gates were open and several children were playing about on the threshold.

'The stockade's complete now,' Master Brewster said, 'Forty miles of fencing, Mistress Joy, with three gateways. That makes us secure from possible attack.'

'Pat—the captain said the Indians were friendly,' Joy said in alarm.

'Too friendly sometimes,' he said ruefully. 'They wander in and out, helping themselves to our supplies whenever they feel like it! But there are always enemies for those of us who seek to worship the Lord in our own way. And I must confess that even within our little community there are sometimes differences of opinion. But here is Peregrine himself, come to meet us!'

He waved his arm and hurried forward while Joy followed, her feet unaccountably dragging. The figure emerging from the open gate was

82

tall and fair haired, clad in sober doublet and breeches, sleeves rolled to his elbows. She thought that she would have remembered him without prompting, but it was hard to be certain. He looked older and harder, and the expression on his face savoured more of surprise then pleasure.

'Mistress Joy-in-the-Lord!' He had reached her and stood staring at her. In one hand he held a long-handled rake and she guessed, from the smears of dirt on his forearms, that he had just come from gardening.

'Master Peregrine.' She raised her eyes to his face and was struck by sudden, paralysing shyness. Beyond Peregrine she could see Patrick who had paused and half turned to watch their meeting.

'This is a—surprise.' He spoke with an effort. 'I had no idea that you would arrive so soon.'

'Captain O'Farrell offered me passage on the *Bridget*' she explained. 'It saved my having to risk an autumn voyage.'

'Yes. Yes, that was most sensible.' He shifted the rake to the other hand and took a step forward, leaning to kiss her cheek. With a squawk of disapproval Polly soared up from her shoulder, crying harshly, 'Damn my eyes! Well, damn my eyes!'

'What,' said Peregrine, 'is *that*?'

'It's a parrot,' Joy said. 'Surely you've seen a parrot before.'

'Yes, of course.' Frowning slightly he stepped back and began to pace slowly at her side as they entered the stockade. 'To whom does it belong?'

'Captain O'Farrell gave her to me as a—a wedding gift,' Joy said, whistling the bird back to her shoulder. 'Her name's Polly and she's very tame. You don't mind our having a pet, do you?'

'No, of course not,' he said hastily. 'There are many cats and dogs around the place, but a bird? And a bird with such language!'

'She learned it aboard ship,' Joy said, and gave a nervous giggle.

Others were hurrying to greet them now. She had a confused impression of an unpaved street with timber-framed houses down each side of it and fenced plots of land between each building. They looked solid, even a trifle weather-beaten, and there were vegetables springing in neat rows beyond the fences.

'Joy!' Her hands were seized and she was whirled about. 'You remember me, don't you?'

'Martha Ford! Of course I remember you!' Joy returned her embrace.

'I'm Martha Browne now. I wed Peter Browne—you remember the Brownes?'

'Yes. Yes, indeed.'

'And you're going to marry Peregrine Carver,' another girl said. 'This is a year for weddings, isn't it?'

'Fear Brewster is taking John Allerton,'

84

Sarah Goodright said. 'He's widowed with three children but Fear was always fond of children. Did you really travel all alone on the *Bridget*? I would never have had such courage!'

Surrounded by chattering companions she was bustled up a narrow pathway into one of the timbered houses. The men had gone on ahead, presumably to discuss business, and Peregrine had gone with them. She wished that he had not relinquished her quite so easily.

'Joy, what a wonderful surprise!' She was being engulfed in another pair of maternal arms.

'Mistress Fenton, how good to see you!' Joy returned the embrace heartily. 'I have a letter for you from Aunt Hepzibah. It's in my trunk somewhere.'

'Your trunk's being carried in,' Sarah Goodright said.

'Oh, it's Mick! Mick is going to settle in the Community if Patrick can buy him an apprenticeship,' Joy said eagerly, turning to greet him.

Mick, setting down the trunk, looked around the small, whitewashed chamber and observed cheerfully.

'Near as a cabin as I ever saw! Captain Patrick said to leave the trunk here until you give word where you want it.'

'That's fine, Mick.' She smiled at him awkwardly as he went out again.

'What a rough-looking boy!' Mistress

Fenton exclaimed. 'Is he one of the crew?'

'He's hoping to settle here as an apprentice. He doesn't have any family,' Joy evaded.

'Well, that will have to be for Governor Bradford to decide,' Mistress Fenton said. 'Now you'll be wanting to wash and change your dress. You have a best gown brought?'

'Yes.'

'This one is stained with seawater and the lace on your coif is quite limp.' Her hostess was bustling her into another room. 'I'll have hot water brought for you in a moment! That parrot—do you have a cage for it?'

'Polly's tame. she doesn't like cages,' Joy said, shooing Polly to the back of the chair where she settled, head under her wing.

'I didn't know Aunt Hepzibah had a parrot,' Mistress Fenton was continuing.

'Patrick O'Farrell gave her to me,' Joy said.

'Captain O'Farrell gave you a present?' The other looked faintly disapproving.

'A wedding present,' Joy said, wishing Mistress Fenton would go away and stop fussing, wishing that Peregrine would come back and put his arms about her in a warm welcome such as she had dreamed about in the three years she had waited for him to write to her. Then an unwilling grin lifted her mouth. Even without a mirror she knew what a spectacle she must have presented, her long skirt stained with salt, her hair hanging lankly down her back, and the bright green parrot on

86

her shoulder. It was no wonder that a proper young man like Peregrine Carver should look dismayed.

Within half an hour she felt both fresher and prettier, her dark-blue Sunday dress belling out round her neat ankles, the pointed collar of white lawn flattering her slim neck. She had brushed her hair until it shone and wound some coloured ribbons through it, and her face was rosy after the soap and water she had applied.

When she came into the outer room she was immediately surrounded by her friends again, all anxious for news from Leyden, all eager to tell her their own news.

'Such a scandal as there has been! Pastor Lyford has been banished these past three months for writing the most dreadful lies about us. We all thought that he was such a pleasant man, but it turned out that in his last ministry he gave advice to betrothed couples and, under cover of that, he—you know!'

'Know what?' Joy enquired.

'The girl told her husband after they were wed, and Pastor Lyford had to leave in a great hurry. It was the most terrible shock to poor Master Brewster!'

'These are not matters to be discussed among unmarried girls,' Mistress Fenton said severely. 'There is to be a feast in honour of the ship's coming, so we are to go to the meeting house. Joy, my dear, we have a tiny room

87

under the eaves where you are most welcome to stay until your marriage.'

'You're very kind,' Joy began, but the older woman waved aside her gratitude.

'Now that Susan is wed the room is spare. It will be good to have someone sleep in it again. There are more houses being built all the time and more people joining us all the time too! This is going to be a fine town one day.'

They went down the path into the unpaved street. Other's were joining them, the ladies in hastily donned best dresses, the men carrying muskets.

'There is a rule that every man must go armed, save when he is in his own home,' Patience Favell whispered, coming to Joy's side. 'If you ask me it's a foolish rule, for we are never attacked and half the muskets don't fire anyway! But 'tis the rule.'

'Is that the meeting house?' Joy asked.

'We all slept there when we first came,' Elizabeth Diz said, 'while the houses were being built and the land shared out. In two ong partitions, the men on one side and the w en on the other, and no more than blankets hung between them!'

'The meeting house is used for special occasions now,' Patience said. 'The Governor's house is built next to it, right on the crossroads. The four guns from the Mayflower are mounted there, to remind us of our beginnings, and the church is there too, only we must call it a prayer-house now.'

Joy's attention had been diverted. At the long low building with the four cannon mounted at its corners stood Master Brewster and a short, thick set man with flaming red hair. That was obviously Miles Standish but her eyes had flown to the tall, black-haired man who leaned against the wall, his arms folded, smiling at her as she approached.

'Mistress Joy.' He bowed slightly as she reached him.

'Captain O'Farrell.' She bent her own head, a smile tugging the corners of her mouth. She couldn't repress the surge of pleasure that rose up in her at the sight of him.

'You're with your friends, I see.' He cocked an eyebrow at the other girls who hung back, fingers twining in their small white aprons, eyelids fluttering coyly down.

'Mistress Elizabeth, and Patience, and Sarah, and this is Mistress Fenton,' Joy said as that lady came panting up.

'Ladies, we must take our places,' Mistress Fenton said, acknowledging Patrick's bow with a somewhat flurried curtsy, her plump face scarlet. 'Captain O'Farrell, it's a very great pleasure to see you again.'

'She said that as if she didn't mean it at all,' Joy said blankly, hanging back as the others were hustled within.

'My reputation has probably run on ahead of me,' Patrick said wryly. 'A Papist sea captain who comes and goes as the wind beckons is a heady brew to set before a gaggle of girls! Where's Polly?'

'Shut in Mistress Fenton's back room! I forgot about her!' She clapped her hand over her mouth in dismay.

'There won't be much left of the furnishings by the time you get back,' Patrick informed her. 'She doesn't take kindly to being shut in strange places.'

'I'll go and fetch her.' Joy turned and sped back down the street.

To her surprise she found Patrick at her side, his long legs taking one step to every two of her own.

'Did you fix a good price for the cargo you brought?' she slowed to ask.

'Less than I wanted to take but more than they wanted to pay, so we are all satisfied,' he told her. 'I've bought an apprenticeship for Mick too, with Perseverance Lee. I know Lee to be a fair man who'll not be over harsh with the lad.'

'He would prefer to sail with you,' Joy reminded him.

'He'll be equally eager to stay here once he's had a taste of land,' Patrick said. 'It's a bad thing for a lad to get too attached to one way of life or one person.'

There it came again, like a warning—his refusal to bind or be bound.

They had reached Mistress Fenton's house

90

and she hastened within to be greeted by Polly's harsh, 'Damn us all! Taking a stroll, my dear?'

'Don't scowl at me,' Patrick said equably when she came out with the bird on her shoulder. 'Polly learned to talk before I obtained her.'

'I shall teach her to sing psalms,' Joy told him.

'I wager you could do it too!' He held open the little picket gate for her. 'You're a resourceful body, Mistress Jones! There are not many maids who would come so far alone to marry—' He paused, glancing down at her, and she said quickly, the colour rising in her face.

'To marry the man I love.'

'As you say.' His smile was downslanting and in exasperation she exclaimed.

'What is it you want of me? You draw me near and then thrust me away, telling me that you have no faith in any woman. I cannot follow your moods!'

'Sometimes I cannot follow them myself,' he said lightly. 'In my experience I've found most women to be false and fickle.'

'I am not!' she began and stopped short, remembering how eagerly she had responded to Patrick's advances when she was on her way to marry another man.

'You are very young,' he said in a more kindly tone, 'and I was in the wrong to seek to

91

take advantage of that, but I wonder if you truly know your own mind. To marry without love in a strange land is not a fate I'd wish on you!'

'I do love Master Carver,' she said, quickening her step. 'In three years my feelings have not altered.'

'But the colour of his eyes has,' Patrick said.

'What?' They were almost at the meeting house but she fixed her eyes on him in bewilderment.

'Master Carver has grey eyes, not blue ones,' Patrick said. 'I took the trouble to notice.'

He had swung past before she could answer. It was just like him, she thought indignantly, to make a remark that left her doubting herself again.

'Mistress Joy, the Grace is to be said! You had better make haste!'

Mistress Fenton had come out to the step and was beckoning her. Joy bit her lip, and hurried within to be met by long rows of heads turned to stare at her direction.

The long wooden building had tables and benches placed down its length. The tables were piled with dishes of food and the benches were crammed with people, many of them old acquaintances from Leyden. Master Brewster stepped forward to shake her hand again and a place was being made for her among the women. She glimpsed Peregrine, too far away for her to examine the exact colour of his eyes,

92

and then Master Brewster began the Grace.

Under cover of the petition she stole a glance from beneath her lowered lashes towards Patrick. He too sat among the men, his garments a splash of brilliant colour against the sober dress of his companions, but his black head was bent and her glance was not returned. '—and bless this food to our use and us to Thy service, Amen,' finished Master Brewster.

'And damn us all, my dears!' Polly squawked loudly. The raucous voice, following on Master Brewster's gentle tone, startled Joy into a peal of mirth. The contrast struck her as so irresistibly comic that it took her a moment to realise that, apart from a few stifled giggles among the younger people, the interruption had been greeted by dead silence. Patrick had his hand across his mouth so that his expression was hidden, but the look on Peregrine's face made her want to laugh all over again.

'Mistress, we must try to turn your pet into a God-fearing bird,' Master Brewster said.

His voice was solemn, but the corners of his mouth twitched slightly.

'I shall do my best, sir,' Joy answered, choking back her laughter, 'but she is very ill-reared, I'm afraid!'

'By a seaman as rough as myself,' Patrick drawled. 'I'm sure that Mistress Joy will do her utmost to convert the creature.'

There was a general clatter of knives and spoons and conversation became general. Patrick had turned to the red-headed Standish at his side and Joy turned her own attention to her meal which, considering it had been produced at such short notice, was both tasty and plentiful.

'We had a good harvest last year,' Patience said, indicating the heaped platters of meat and fruit, the basket of corn bread. 'This year will be better, they say, unless the frost comes soon.'

'It will taste even better after the food aboard ship,' Elizabeth assured her.

'Oh, it was not so bad,' Joy bit thoughtfully into an apple.

'Were you very sick? I almost died of seasickness when we came over,' Sarah leaned to say. 'Mind you, we had a dreadful passage and arrived in winter.'

'I wasn't sick.'

'But you must have been afraid,' Sarah persisted. 'To be all alone among a crew of sailors, and not even a pastor on board!'

'I never felt the lack of one,' Joy confessed frankly.

It was the wrong thing to say. She had no sooner uttered the words when she sensed a withdrawal in their manner. Sarah, her tone virtuous, said after a moment.

'They say that the observance of the faith is somewhat neglected in Leyden and that our people are picking up bad habits from the Dutch.'

'I don't think Joy will have picked up any bad habits,' Patience said kindly.

'Sometimes I think bad habits are more fun than good ones,' Joy said naughtily and, in the midst of another awkward little silence, munched on the apple and offered Polly a piece.

Master Brewster was banging a gavel on the table and the talk was stilled.

'Fellow citizens, this is a joyful occasion,' he was announcing. 'We have books and woollen goods for the winter and another supply ship due in October or November. And we have Mistress Joy-in-the-Lord here among us to marry one of our respected young men. We also have another newcomer to swell our ranks. The boy Mick, who is an orphan, has been bound apprentice to Master Lee for a period not exceeding three years and we welcome him heartily among us. To mark this occasion, when you have all eaten your fill we will make haste to the prayer-house to sing praise to the Lord for all the good things He has bestowed upon us. Captain O'Farrell, you would be most welcome to join us.'

He glanced hopefully towards Patrick who set down his mug of ale and answered, courteously but hastily.

'I have to be on my way, Master Brewster! I'm taking the longboat up river to the

Algonquin village. I have some fishing and hunting to catch up on.'

'I wish you a pleasant stay then, and hope one day to persuade you to join us in our worship,' the older man said.

'Master Brewster, if any man were to persuade me into your meeting it would be yourself,' Patrick said.

'Another time perhaps,' Master Brewster smiled in resignation.

The meal was nearly finished. Joy drank her own ale and rose with the other girls.

'You are not thinking of bringing that bird into the prayer-house, are you?' Peregrine asked, coming to her from his place among the men.

He had washed the dirt from himself and looked fresh and handsome. He was much more handsome than Patrick O'Farrell, she thought, and she found that her eyes had slid past him towards the captain.

'Mistress? I asked you about the bird,' Peregrine repeated, his cool tone sharpening.

'Oh, I'll leave Polly outside,' Joy said. Patrick was clapping Mick on the shoulder and striding out, not even glancing at her. 'She's probably a Papist bird anyway!'

CHAPTER EIGHT

'Peregrine is here,' Mistress Fenton said, putting her head in at the door where Joy sat finishing a late breakfast.

She had been left to sleep until mid-morning though her hostess had informed her that most people rose with the dawn.

'Up with the sun and to bed soon after the sun goes down,' she said. 'In summer the days are most long and pleasant and it's good to do one's work in the sunshine.'

Joy had slept only fitfully though the room under the eaves was clean and bright. She had woken several times, wondering at the silence that pressed around her. She had grown accustomed to the swinging of the lantern on its hook, the wailing of the wind as it tore through the rigging, the slap of the water against the bows as the *Bridget* sailed on. This tiny room was too peaceful and too still. She pushed aside the covers and fell into a dreaming sleep where she climbed up the side of a tall ship towards Patrick O'Farrell. The dream was so vivid that she could smell the sea and feel the rungs of the vertical ladder beneath her feet, but as she neared the top she saw that it was Peregrine who waited to receive her.

It had been a relief to wake fully and descend into the main part of the house. Master Fenton was already out fishing with a party of other men, his wife informed her.

'And Governor Bradford went hunting two days since and we expect him back soon,' Mistress Fenton continued. 'He is a most excellent man and a fine leader. Today you must feel free to explore the Settlement, my dear, and not think of helping me. Help will be welcome when you are settled in.'

She nodded and smiled as she bustled about setting the room to rights. There was not much to tidy up. The furnishings were sparse and the square of braided matting had been washed so often that it had lost most of its colour.

Peregrine, tapping on the door as Mistress Fenton opened it, was clad in his sober church-going doublet, his fair hair neatly combed. He stooped to kiss Joy's cheek, and she felt his lips tight and cool on her skin before he straightened up and said, 'With your permission, Mistress Fenton, I will take Joy to look at my house.'

'I'll get my cloak.' Joy rose, reaching for it from the hook on the wall and whistling to Polly who, having spent the night at the foot of the bed, now perched on the back of a chair, grumbling to herself.

'You will need your coif,' he reminded her, glancing at her uncovered head.

She put it on obediently, tying the ribbons under her chin, and went out into the sunlit street as Peregrine held open the door for them.

'It really is becoming like a town!' She stood at the gate, looking about her at the timbered houses, each with its plot of land. There were children skipping in the road and several boys were chopping logs in a cleared space.

'One day it will be a fine city.' Peregrine answered her confidently. 'The streets will be paved and there will be a school and a court-house and roads leading to the next town. There are settlements springing up all down the coast as the forests are cleared and more ships risk the long voyage to trade with the New World!'

'Where is your house?' she asked eagerly as they walked down the street.

'This way.' He guided her to the left. 'The town was planned in the form of a cross and every person given an equal measure of land, so larger households have bigger gardens. Although I am unmarried I was allowed sufficient ground for two because of my intention to wed you.' It crossed her mind that families didn't stay the same size as old people died and babes were born, but he was waxing so enthusiastically on the advantages of the settlement that she didn't like to interrupt.

'There is game here in abundance and much fishing. Herring and cod mainly, but trout and salmon in the rivers and shellfish such as we never got in Leyden. We grow corn and beans too, and there is a bird we call a turkey that is bigger and fatter than any bird you ever saw!

This is the house I've built.'

He spoke up proudly as if he had erected the building all by himself, Joy thought. To her it looked exactly the same as all the others, its roof shingled, its doors whitewashed, a short path leading up from the fence gate.

'We have oiled paper in the windows to cut down the glare of the sun, and wooden shutters for the winter and the nights,' he pointed out. 'I have two cows which is unusual for a single man, but when my uncle, Governor Carver, died he left his cow to me.'

'I was sorry to hear of his death,' Joy said.

'Only a few days after I landed here, and my poor aunt followed him not six weeks later. There were many died in those first two or three years. Must you bring that bird inside?' His tone had sharpened again and the look he threw at Polly was distinctly irritated.

'I'll leave her on the fence.' A trifle hurt at the abruptness of his tone Joy set Polly on the top of the fence staves and followed him within.

'Four rooms, as I said in my letter,' Peregrine said. 'A living room with a kitchen behind and two bed-chambers above. It would not be fitting for you to see them yet.'

'For heaven's sake, why not?' Joy demanded, her foot already on the ladder. 'I'll be sleeping in one of them when we're wed!'

'We are not yet wed,' he said stiffly. 'Besides there is nought up there but a bed and a washstand in each room.'

'And you fear your passion will overcome you when you see me and the bed together,' she said laughing.

'Mistress, I wish you would not jest so coarsely,' he said, not joining her in her laughter. 'I know you mean no harm but it adds to the bad impression.'

'Adds to?' Her laughter stilled, she raised her eyes to his grave face. 'Adds to?'

'You have not been very circumspect since your arrival,' he said, looking acutely uncomfortable.

'In what way have I not been "very circumspect"?' Her blue eyes glinted but her voice was honey sweet. Deep within her a spark of temper glowed.

'To sail alone in the first place,' he began.

'Not exactly alone,' she interrupted. 'Patrick O'Farrell had a crew of ten.'

'O'Farrell is a Papist. It is a shame that we must trade with such men.'

'His beliefs are his own business. We never talked of such matters,' she said loftily.

'You must have talked about something,' Peregrine said. 'You were not struck dumb for the entire voyage, were you? He must have enjoyed your conversation since he gave you a present.'

'Gave *us* a present! Polly is a wedding gift to us both.'

'And one we could have done without, judging from the language the creature uses!'

His face had paled and his eyes—they *were* grey!—were cold. 'You cannot be so lost to all sense that you don't know how embarrassed I was, how embarrassed everybody was, when you came late to the meal with your hair unbound and a swearing parrot on your shoulder!'

She stared at him, her temper dying into misery, and heard herself say, 'We're quarrelling. I've not been a full day here and we're quarrelling.'

'I don't mean to quarrel,' he said. 'I want to be proud of the woman I marry, that's all.'

'Then you should be proud of me!' Her rage flared again. 'I came on an earlier vessel, to surprise you. There was a storm and I was nearly washed overboard. Perhaps you're sorry that I wasn't, then I couldn't have walked in with Polly and embarrassed you! Or did you never stop to think of how it was for me, coming so far and you looking at me as if I were something the cat dragged in?'

'I wanted everything to be ready for you,' he protested.

'It looks ready enough now.' She swept her arm about the room. 'You're living here, aren't you? You've beds and stools and dishes and two cows on your own plot of land!'

'Sarah wanted to make it pretty for you,' he said.

'Sarah who?' Joy asked bluntly.

'Sarah Goodright. She has been helping me

102

to make the house pleasant for a wife to live in,' he explained. 'She has made some curtains and a cloth for the table and almost finished plaiting a rug. It was going to be quite perfect by the time you arrived.'

'Oh.' Suddenly deflated, Joy sat down on a stool and gazed at him.

'There would have been a fire to warm you,' Peregrine said, 'and pies cooling in the larder.'

'And I ruined it all by arriving out of season. Peregrine, you're glad to see me, despite all that, aren't you?' she pleaded. 'Say that you're glad to see me! Why, you've not even embraced me yet and surely that's proper now that we're betrothed!'

'Yes, of course.' His expression had softened as he drew her into his arms, pressing his mouth on her mouth. She kissed him back, her body yielding as she waited for the familiar trembling to begin, but the embrace was over too soon. Holding her hands he said, smilingly.

'You have grown into a pretty young woman. When I left you had the promise of beauty but it was not yet there. Three years have made a great difference.'

'An improvement?' she enquired teasingly.

'All good things improve. When we are married and you feel more settled here you will be even prettier.' He kissed her again, on the cheek. 'I had forgotten that your eyes were blue.'

'And I had forgotten that yours were not.'

103

'I beg your pardon?' he said puzzled.

'Never mind. It's not important.' She smiled at him, feeling as if she had just closed something in a box and shut it away at the back of her mind. 'Oh, Peregrine, this is a lovely house! You have made it so fine! Truly, I never saw a finer!'

'It is sturdy enough,' he said deprecatingly, but he looked pleased. 'Some of the furniture I inherited from my aunt, but the rest I made. Sarah is making some cushions for the chairs.'

'What colour?'

'Red, I think. Red was always one of Sarah's favourite colours. The curtains have a fringe along the bottom of them,' he said.

'Well, it will look very cheerful,' she said kindly.

'I have a churn,' he said, 'so you can start making butter and cheese as soon as we are wed. Did you bring any thread for the making of lace?'

'A box of it.'

'Lace edgings are still fashionable among the younger maids, so we can make a profit,' he said.

'Yes. We have our living to earn,' she agreed. 'Aunt Hepzibah gave me seeds too and some ointment for the making of salves.'

'We shall prosper!' He caught her hand again and drew her back within the circle of his arm. 'The Lord blesses the righteous with prosperity!'

104

'And with love?' She looked up at him wistfully. 'There will be love as well as profit in our marriage, won't there?'

'Love grows over the years like a plant growing in the field,' he said.

'Yes,' she said meekly, while inside her something protested, 'But it's not always so! Love can strike like lightning, twisting your heart and blinding your eyes'.

'Come and look at the garden. I have corn, peas and beans flourishing,' he invited. 'We won't go short this winter. Indeed we'll have sufficient to barter for something else of which we have need.'

He led her to the back of the house where she stood, looking down a long, narrow enclosed plot of land in which vegetables marched like sentinels.

'The soil is good but not deep, and one needs to keep the weeds back,' Peregrine said.

'There are no flowers,' Joy said.

'Flowers? One cannot eat flowers,' he smiled.

'They look pretty.'

'There are plenty of wild blossoms in the woods and meadows, if that's your fancy,' he told her. 'There are nut trees grow there too. The women go to gather them.'

'Where are your cows? What do you call them?'

'They graze on the commonland,' he said. 'I never thought of giving the beasts names but—'

'I shall call them—'

'Sarah named them Yield Well and Give Much,' he continued, ignoring her. 'I thought it was an amusing conceit. What else did you bring with you?'

'A quilt made of patchwork—'

'Sarah has made a splendid quilt!' he broke in. 'She is a most skilled needlewoman. If you ask her she will likely help you with your wedding gown.'

'It's made,' Joy said curtly. 'I can sew a little myself, you know.'

'Of course you can,' he said. 'Don't forget that I have seen your lace. When you were a child you could weave the most exquisite patterns that would fetch a good price even then.'

'Let's walk in the woods!' She let his hand loose and sped down the path, her skirt belling out round her ankles. 'Come and walk in the woods with me, Peregrine! There are gates in the stockade, aren't there?'

'Yes, of course, but there are no more nut-gathering parties until after the Sabbath,' he said.

'I don't want to gather nuts.' She ran back, seizing his arm and pressing it to her side. 'I don't want to do anything useful or profitable! I simply want to walk and maybe run, dance!'

'You're not making sense.'

'Do we have to make sense always?' she

106

asked. 'Cannot we talk nonsense in an idle hour?'

'Didn't Miss Hepzibah tell you that idle hours are there for the devil to fill?' he said indulgently.

'Aunt Hepzibah is in Leyden and we are here in the New World,' she said impatiently.

'Which makes it the more important that we keep up all the standards on which we base our lives,' Peregrine said.

'We're not children,' she argued.

'But, God willing, we will be an example to children of our own,' he said. 'Dear Mistress Joy, how could we hope to rear our children in the Lord's grace if we cannot control our own instincts?'

'But we're not even married yet!' she protested. 'You talks as if we were middle-aged with a brood of younglings!'

'You want my children, don't you?' he said anxiously.

'Oh, a dozen at least!' she said flippantly, whirling away from him and snapping off a peapod.

'Four would be more sensible. Two boys and two girls, though that's not in our choosing.'

'Peregrine, I was jesting! I don't want a dozen children!' she exclaimed. 'I've never even considered how many I *do* want! Some, I suppose, in due time, but let us think of the wedding first. When is it to be?'

'I had planned for the beginning of

November, when your ship arrived.' 'But I came sooner,' she reminded him. 'Could we not make it sooner?'

'October, Perhaps.' He put out his hand to straighten her coif. 'I think I could make all ready in time for October.'

'October then.' She smiled, forbearing to mention that six weeks lay ahead before October came.

Peregrine had grown solemn and serious, she thought, or perhaps he had always been so and she had forgotten.

'Come and I'll show you the byre,' he said. 'I built it close against the house for the winters here are harsh.'

'But it's summer now! The sun is shining and your vegetables are shooting up into the sky and the house is beautiful!' she cried.

'I'm glad you're pleased,' he began, but she was speeding round to the front of the house again, whistling to Polly who landed on her with a little digging of claws as if to punish her in some fancied neglect. Peregrine, following more slowly, said, the impatience edging his voice again, 'That bird will require a cage.'

'Polly's never been in a cage. She had a perch on the *Bridget*, but she can balance anywhere,' Joy informed him. 'She can fly too. Her wings were never clipped.'

'Does she fly far?' he asked hopefully.

'I don't think she ever has. If you like she can sleep in the byre with the cows,' Joy offered.

'Damn that for a tale!' Polly shrieked, fluttering away again.

'I could swear she understood every word people said,' Joy declared, hiding a smile as she saw Peregrine's face.

'That's not possible,' he said flatly. 'Birds imitate the human voice, which is why this one uses such foul speech. I hope that you were not exposed to such talk when you were aboard ship.'

'Patrick threatened his crew with dire penalties if he caught them swearing.'

'You call him Patrick.'

'I didn't call him anything much.' The colour had risen in her face. 'But his crew were all most respectful!'

'One would hope so,' Peregrine said. There was a little frown between his eyes but she ignored it, tucking her arm through his as they began to walk up the street again.

'Tell me what do you do with yourself all day,' she invited.

'The work takes up most of the day,' he said. 'In a new land there is so much to be done! Each man devotes a certain portion of his time in helping to clear the forest and build new houses or repair the ones already built. Then we have our own crops to tend, hunting, fishing, and of course there is a musket practice which every man is obliged to attend.'

'It's a wonder you can fit in time for a wedding,' Joy said.

There was a slight snap in her voice but Peregrine didn't seem to notice as he replied amiably.

'We shall take the entire day, simply to celebrate the event and enjoy ourselves with our friends. Weren't you happy to see so many familiar faces when you arrived?'

'Yes indeed,' she assured him.

'The Governor hopes that we can earn sufficient from our trade in fish and furs to pay the passage of those still in Holland,' he told her. 'In another ten years this will be exactly like Leyden.'

'Shouldn't it be like a new country, otherwise we might as well have stayed in Leyden?' she objected.

'Here we can worship in freedom with no danger of the Spaniards invading,' he said. 'Mistress Hepzibah would be most happy if she could bring herself to make the journey, and you would be happier if she came, wouldn't you?'

'I'm happy to be with you,' Joy said impulsively. 'When a girl weds she leaves her home behind surely!'

'But I would feel happier if your aunt had been with you on the voyage,' he fretted. 'At least she would have been company for you.'

It sounded reasonable enough, but Joy had the feeling that it was as chaperone he would have welcomed Aunt Hepzibah as a passenger on the *Bridget*. The little touch of jealousy

110

ought to have flattered her but she could only feel acutely uncomfortable.

CHAPTER NINE

There had been the usual Thursday Prayer meeting at which Governor Bradford had been welcomed back from his hunting trip and Joy, who had known him only by sight, presented to him.

'Mistress, this is a very great pleasure.' He had taken her hand in a warm, firm clasp and smiled at her kindly in a way that made her understand why Mistress Fenton had praised him so highly to her.

'A most excellent leader of men for all that he is still only in his thirties! He is a man of great good sense in whom we all trust. You know, of course, of his great tragedy?'

'His wife drowned, did she not?'

'A few days after our first landing. Poor Dorothy! It was said that she had a dizzy spell and fell from the ship into the harbour. There were others who said privately that she had been in a state of deep depression for many days. It was not talked about openly of course. However he has married again and Alice is a most loving wife, so all ends well,' Mistress Fenton said, brushing aside tragedy as briskly as she would have swept dust over the threshold of her spotless little house.

Now William Bradford pressed Joy's hand and half turned to clap Peregrine on the shoulder.

'You are to be congratulated, my friend, on your choice of a bride, and one who comes ahead of her time,' he said heartily. 'When is the wedding to be?'

'In October. The house will be completely ready by then.'

'Ah, yes. Mistress Sarah has been adding the feminine touch that all wives require,' Master Bradford said.

Joy wondered why two intelligent men didn't seem to realise that a wife might like to add her own feminine touch and not have everything done for her by another woman. Peregrine however was smiling and agreeing, and she moved away and fell in with the stream of girls filing out of the Prayer house.

'Joy, did you see the cows that I named?' Sarah Goodright enquired, coming to walk with her. 'Yield Well and Give Much have quite a comic ring, don't you think?'

'Very witty,' Joy said, trying to make her tone warmly cordial but somehow failing.

'And the house? Is it not a marvellous one?'

'Yes. Indeed yes.'

Sarah had fair hair and a round face marred by traces of the smallpox that had attacked her when she was a child. She was about twenty and ought to have been wed by now but her

112

sweetheart had been among those who had died in that first harsh winter. Word of the deaths had been sent back to Leyden and a service of condolence held, but in the four years since she had obviously forgotten her grief and she was all cheerfulness as she slipped her hand into the crook of Joy's arm, saying.

'Oh, but it is so *good* to have someone come from Leyden! We have had no opportunity for a talk yet. You must tell me simply everything that has happened since we met. One cannot put everything into a letter.'

'There is not much to tell.' Joy hesitated, then rushed on awkwardly. 'I am most grateful for all the work you've done—the sewing and the quilting.'

'It was my pleasure,' Sarah said. 'I am very fond of needlework, and it was interesting to plan what ought to go in the house, and to match the colours.'

'Red,' Joy said.

'We had a lot of red woollen stuff brought in the last shipment of supplies and Master Peregrine bought it cheaply,' Sarah prattled on. 'It is fortunate that I am exceedingly partial to the shade so it was no great task for me to sew it.'

'For my own part I am not very partial to the colour,' Joy said. 'It has always made me look sallow.'

'Oh, but I never thought!' Sarah's hand dropped from her arm and she turned a

113

dismayed face towards her. 'I have been so interested in making things ready that I never even stopped to think that you might hate it!'

'I didn't say that I hated it,' Joy began, but Sarah had turned back and was tugging at Peregrine's sleeve, her voice high and remorseful.

'Master Peregrine, how could you let me make red furnishings when Mistress Joy simply hates the colour? Oh, but I could weep to think of all the work wasted. You really should have told me!'

'I didn't know,' Peregrine began in bewilderment, his eyes moving past Sarah's fair head to where Joy stood.

'I don't hate the colour at all!' She had answered too loudly and several heads turned in her direction. 'Sarah has misunderstood me.'

'You said that it made you look sallow,' Sarah whispered. 'Oh, but you are likely right for I had forgotten you are somewhat sallow! It makes no matter for I can use all the things myself if you will allow me to buy them from you.'

'Don't be foolish,' Peregrine said. His voice was comforting and he patted her shoulder as she stared up at him with tear-filled eyes.

'But one cannot expect poor Joy to live with things that make her look sallow,' Sarah wailed.

'Joy doesn't expect to match all the

114

furnishings to her complexion,' Peregrine said. 'Don't be such a goose!'

'Indeed not,' Joy said. 'It has been most kind of you to help, Sarah, and red is—is a most lively shade. In the winter it will make everything seem very warm.'

'Then you don't object to my finishing? There are the cushions and—.'

'How could anyone possibly object to someone helping them so generously?' Peregrine said. 'Dry your eyes, Sarah.'

He spoke with the faint impatience of someone who was not really sure what all the fuss is about, but one or two of those passing turned to look.

'You didn't have to be so mean to poor Sarah,' Elizabeth whispered, coming to Joy's side as they resumed their walk. 'She has been so excited about your coming and she hoped her work would be a surprise for you.'

'I wasn't!' Joy protested. 'I'm truly grateful for her kindness.'

The thought that it was a little harsh to be put so thoroughly in the wrong flashed through her mind but she put it firmly aside and said, her voice raised a little.

'I think Sarah has been most kind and generous. Truly I cannot thank her sufficiently for the trouble she has taken!'

'I did what I could.' Sarah dabbed at her eyes and managed a watery smile. 'It would have been finished if you had not sailed on an earlier ship.'

115

'Perhaps you would like me to turn around again and go back and come again in November?' Joy couldn't resist saying.

Sarah laughed, but Peregrine looked faintly annoyed as he joined them and they began to drift off to their various homes.

'You're in a strange mood,' he said. 'I never knew you so prickly before.'

Joy was tempted to retort that he had never known her before, but the unhappy expression on his face softened her.

'I am out of temper,' she said lightly. 'Pray take no notice. Probably the sermon was too long.'

'It lasted less than two hours,' he said.

'But it's the third I've sat through in three days,' she pointed out. 'There was a Thanksgiving for my safe arrival and yesterday the children's Service and this morning the Prayer Meeting proper—I am quite stiff with sitting still!'

'I thought the sermon an interesting one,' he said, unmollified. 'The way that Master Brewster likened the governor's hunting to the Lord's snaring of souls was very neat.'

'Cannot we enjoy ourselves for a while now?' She slipped her hand into his and tried to smooth down her ruffled feelings.

'Nothing would please me more but I'm behindhand with the work as it is,' he said.

'Oh.' She withdrew her hand, disappointment clouding her face.

116

'Don't you think Mistress Fenton would appreciate a helping hand?' he said after a moment.

'Or I could help Sarah with her sewing,' Joy said.

'She'd be glad to have your company.'

He had completely missed the snap in her voice and there was relief in his tone as he nodded smilingly and went off in the direction of the house.

Our house, Joy corrected herself as she stood staring after him. He built it for me and Sarah has gone to great trouble to make it all nice, and I have done nothing but grumble and make objections. He will think me grown into a scold.

She strolled on down the street. It was a fine, warm day and many of the women now brushing their steps had rolled up their sleeves. She could, she supposed, go back and help Mistress Fenton, but her hostess was one of those women who never think a task done properly unless they have done it themselves. All around her the sights and sounds of the morning's city. The noise of splintering wood came from the small lumber yard; a woman washing looked up from a tub of steaming water to smile at her, two boys went past driving a cow to pasture. The Settlement was thriving and its citizens busy and it was impossible to walk very far in any direction without seeing the high wooden stockade.

Impulsively she changed direction, making her way towards one of the open gates. It was, after all, high summer and if Peregrine was too busy to escort her on a walk then she saw no reason why she shouldn't go alone.

The grass that stretched around the fence was starred with flowers as thickly as tapestry and the trees were carpeted in moss. She gained their shelter, and looked up through a tracery of beech and hawthorn branches into blue space across which an occasional white cloud drifted. There was a sense of freedom in the air such as she had not sensed in the unpaved streets and neat, wooden houses, and her step became a skip as she went on. The nuts were already ripe, hanging in gleaming clusters within her reach. She bit her lip, wishing that she had remembered to get a basket, and then pulled off her coif, swinging it by the ribbons as she darted from tree to tree. The nuts were sweet. She cracked several between her teeth and chewed them with relish. The woods were growing thicker, and more than once she had to stop and pull aside the creepers that impeded her path. The paths themselves were becoming narrower and once she came up short against a high hedge of thorn starred with white flowers.

She had to search for a while before she found a way around it, but beyond that was a glade fragrant with bushes of wild lavender, a

118

brook meandering through it. It was one of the loveliest spots she had ever seen and, for a few moments, she stood, watching in delight, as a thin-legged fawn bent its head to the water and drank.

A slight movement or a sound must have startled the beast for it raised its sleek head on the long neck and bounded into the thicket again. Joy emerged from concealment and knelt down in the rushes that bordered the stream, cupping her hands to drink the cold, fresh water that tingled in her mouth like wine. The long grass was soft, glinted with sunshine, and she sat back, eating the rest of the nuts and amusing herself by floating the little curving shells down the fast-flowing stream. If Aunt Hepzibah were here she would be shocked at such idleness, and talk a great deal about parents turning over in graves. Joy laughed aloud, stretching her arms over her head. All about her were the little sounds of woodland, the rustling of some shy creature making for its burrow, the song of a lark high among the trees. The birdsong reminded her that she had better be getting back to feed Polly. She had bowed to the general opinion and shut the bird in her room before setting out for the Prayer Meeting, it being agreed that Polly's raucous comments didn't exactly add to the spiritual quality of the occasion. By now Polly would be hungry and bad-tempered. Joy was beginning to feel empty herself, nuts and spring water being an inadequate substitute for a good meal. She tied on her coif, plucked the blades of grass off her skirt and began, somewhat reluctantly, to retrace her steps.

Peregrine's opinion of her would most certainly drop if he ever knew that she had been wasting her time in such a fashion. With this in mind she stepped aside to pick some gold-eyed daises that sprang in a large clump between two spreading beeches. At least she would provide herself with an excuse for leaving the stockade in the first place.

She had gathered a generous bouquet, too many for her to hold even in both hands, and spent further minutes in pulling some threads from her skirt and binding them tightly round the stems. By the time this task was completed the sun had risen even higher, blazing down on the grass. It was a relief to be on the narrow path that wound between the trees again. There was a welcome shade here and she slowed her pace, breathing in the damp, cool scent of the moss.

There was no sign of the thorn hedge she had skirted previously. In some way she must have taken the wrong path when she stepped aside to pluck the daises. She turned back, following the splashing of water that would, she hoped, lead her back into the glade. It led instead to a pool surrounded by rocks down which the water was splashing and, when she had squeezed past them, the path wound on into a wilderness of trees that loomed against the sunlit sky in a manner that struck her as faintly menacing.

It was stupid to feel a queer, panicky sensation low in her stomach. Joy stood, clutching the flowers, forcing herself to take several deep breaths. In a moment she would get her bearings and start back, so there was no sense in being afraid. She couldn't have wandered very far from the stockade. She turned around slowly, trying to remember which way she had come. Her wisest plan was probably to clamber up the rocks and try to glimpse the course of the stream below, but she found it impossible to get a secure foothold on the slippery stone. She tried again, dropping her flowers in the process, and finally gave up the attempt in disgust.

A curving track beyond the pool looked as if it might double back upon itself. She grimaced at it doubtfully, then shrugged her shoulders and stepped out on it, retrieving her blossoms as she went. It certainly turned and twisted, now looping about a tree, now vanishing in a patch of marsh that sucked at her shoes if she hesitated for an instant. She ran for a while and then slowed down, aware of her own foolishness in hurrying when every path she took looked more unfamiliar than the last. The truth was that she was hopelessly confused as to which direction she ought to be going in.

She raised her voice and shouted loudly and unavailingly disturbing a covey of partridges that flew up out of a nearby bush. Their whirring wings startled her so much that she sat down abruptly on a grassy knoll. Her heart was hammering and she was finding it difficult to breathe.

'This,' she said aloud, 'is mere foolishness.' Her voice echoed back to her from the surrounding trees and she felt suddenly alone as she had not felt since entering the woods. It was the first time she had ever been alone with no houses or walls in sight. Even on the ship, in the middle of the heaving ocean, there had been Patrick and the other members of the crew. Here there were only the trees and the unseen creatures that rustled through the undergrowth. The woods were full of game, she reminded herself. It was silly to think of herself as being alone.

She forced herself to rise and walk on. At least it was shady here and soon, surely very soon, they would realise that she was missing from the Settlement! The fear that nobody would was a fear she refused to admit even for a moment. Instead she held on tightly to the rapidly wilting daisies and forced herself to plod on. At least she had the illusion of going somewhere, though the woods were growing more dense, the patches of sunlight smaller and more rare.

She had been walking for hours and the sun

122

was descending the arch of the sky. Joy had been humming, more to keep her spirits up than anything, but her mouth was dry and her stomach so empty that she looked about her hoping to spot something edible. She had left the groves of beech and hazel and the berries on the bushes that straggled across the path were still green. Neither was there any more sign of pool or stream. There were animals here, but she had nothing with which to catch one even if she had the heart to try. It was more likely that one of them would catch her, she thought, her imagination supplying ripping claws and snapping jaws.

There was a worse possibility. She could wander for days, tormented by heat and thirst until she went mad or became exhausted and died of it.

Her legs were aching and her head throbbed. It would be much wiser, she decided, trying to think clearly and logically, to rest for a while. Later, if dusk had fallen and nobody had found her, she would seek some concealed place and stay in it until morning.

If only Patrick were here—she caught herself up short and hastily substituted Peregrine's name. If only Peregrine were here then she would have nothing to fear. Stifling a sob she let herself slip down, her back against a tree, the browning petals in her hands blurring as tears filled her eyes and began to slide down her cheeks.

CHAPTER TEN

It was impossible to know whether she was going towards the Settlement or away from it. The sun, she reminded herself, set in the west, but she was so disorientated that she couldn't remember in which region the stockade had been built. It was growing chillier, the heat of the day withdrawing from the world, the shadows becoming longer and blacker. The woods that had welcomed her now menaced, the long trails of bramble snagging her stockings, the branches shutting out the light. Then, without warning, she pushed her way through a clump of elders and emerged into bare ground. All about her the short grass dipped and rose like the sea, and a cold wind blew across the darkening landscape. Joy shivered, pulling her cloak about herself. The flowers were limp in her hands, their petals falling. Clearly they were blooms that died soon after they were picked, but she hung on to them. At least she was clear of the trees. Here and there the grass gleamed emerald even in the fading light. She put a tentative foot on to it and sank immediately up to the ankle. Bog marsh! She drew back her foot and shuddered. There was no way of telling how far the marsh extended, no way of picking out a path across it. If she turned back she would soon be hopelessly engulfed in the trees once more.

The tears threatened to spill over again. She wiped them away impatiently and raised her chin. Even at the height of the heavy storm she had felt a heady exhilaration, but Patrick had been there. Now she was alone with the night beginning to shroud her and all the imagined terrors of childhood attaining shape and substance.

At the far side of the marsh something leapt into sparkling light and was gone before she could be certain that she had seen anything. It came again, thin tongues of flame reaching up into the sky. Someone was lighting a fire. She ran forward, heedless of the treacherous ground that sucked at her feet. There were darker patches of ground that were firmer. She zigzagged as well as she could from one to the other, frequently slipping, once landing up to her waist in cold mud that lurked below the surface of apparently firm ground. Gasping, she clutched at the nearest tussock of grass and raised her voice in a despairing cry that sounded, in her own ears, pitifully weak. 'Patrick! Patrick O'Farrell! Patrick!'

There were other lights, twinkling and bobbing in a line. She pulled herself on to level ground and yelled again, her voice cracking.

Other voices answered her. The relief, after so many hours, of hearing human beings again was so intense that she was torn between laughter and weeping. Figures strung out across the marsh were coming closer. She recognised Patrick even in the dim light and thought in confusion that there was mud on her skirt and hands. It seemed a foolish thing to worry about but as he dragged her clear of the bog and set her on her feet she found that she was crying, great gulping sobs threatening to tear her apart.

'It's all right.' Patrick was holding her tightly, shaking her a little. 'It's all right now. The Lord knows what the hell you're doing here but it's all right.'

'It isn't! I'm in the most dreadful mess!' She blurted out the words, her tears falling faster, her mouth trembling as she looked up at him.

'Truer word was never spoken,' he said, looking down at her. His own expression was one of tender amusement and, for one glorious instant, she closed her eyes, revelling in the feeling of being cared for and protected. It was gone directly and her eyes flew open in disbelieving fury as he said, 'You deserve to be thrust straight back into that bog! I never met anyone better at being in the wrong place at the wrong time. Can you walk further or do you need to be carried?'

'I can walk anywhere!' Joy said defiantly, and felt her legs buckle beneath her.

Patrick wasted no further words. She was scooped up and hoisted across his broad shoulder in a manner that was distinctly unromantic before he turned, weaving his way

126

with the ease of experience past the marsh grass on a path that twisted towards the flickering lights, calling as he went to the figures who had accompanied him. Joy had a fleeting glance of a coppery face, daubed with streaks of white and purple, and a headdress of bronze feathers. Then she was being set down on solid ground again and Patrick, his arm about her shoulders, was guiding her forward.

There were wicker huts, circular in shape, dotted about a wide clearing with flaming torches stuck in the ground outside the low entrances. She could see Patrick's companions more clearly now. They were tall, reddish-brown men, their hair braided and ornamented with feathers, naked save for breech clouts and short cloaks plentifully decorated with shells and dyed grasses. It was the first time she had seen any natives and, despite her fatigue, she found herself studying them with interest. There were women there too, some with babes in wicker cradles strapped to their backs, their loose one-piece dresses fringed and dyed in a variety of bright colours. They were all chattering in a curious singsong language, pointing at her and then covering their mouths with their hands.

'They'll boil some water for you,' Patrick told her. 'Or is it the fashion in the Settlement now to take mud baths?'

'Don't be so silly! I fell in that bog,' Joy began crossly.

'Well in!' he grinned and gave her a little push in the direction of one of the huts.

Inside it was more roomy than she had expected, with rush mats covering the ground and bowls in which lumps of burning fat floated on oil. Even in their uncertain light she could discern the streaks of mud on her hands and the filthy condition of her skirt. No doubt her face was just as dirty. She was also exceedingly cold.

'Get your dress off and wrap yourself in this blanket until the water's ready,' Patrick said, ducking in after her.

'Do you have to order me about?' she retorted shiveringly.

'No. I can spend an hour persuading you while you catch your death of cold,' he returned. 'Do as I bid you.'

He tossed an evil-smelling blanket towards her and turned his back. She wriggled out of her wet garments and wrapped it about her just as he turned round again.

'Now you look like a fairly respectable squaw,' he commented. 'One of the women will give you a dress when you've scraped off some of this dirt! Meanwhile you'd better eat.'

He stepped aside to where a dish of fruit and a jug of ale were placed.

'Is this your hut?' she asked, accepting the mug of ale and the apple he brought her.

'Wickiup,' he corrected. 'No, it's the guest wickiup. Chief Massasoit keeps it for visitors.

The Algonquins are a hospitable people.'

'This is the Algonquin village? I must have walked miles!' she exclaimed in dismay.

'If you came from the Settlement about eight miles, as the crow flies.'

'I didn't fly,' she said and giggled suddenly.

'That you didn't!' he agreed amiably. 'What possessed you to wander off alone? Did you quarrel with the estimable Master Carver?'

'Indeed not!' She drank more of the ale, her spirits rising. 'I stepped out for a walk in the woods as I have a perfect right to do.'

'Not if you don't know the country,' he said. 'That's as foolish as setting out to sea without a compass!'

'I rush everywhere without a compass,' she said lightly.

'And do you arrive at the place where you want to be?' he enquired.

In the flickering light it was hard to read his expression, but there was a curious stillness about him.

'Yes,' she said flatly, clutching the blanket around herself. 'Yes, I do!'

'Then Master Carver should count himself fortunate that he has a wife who knows where she's going,' he said. 'Ah! here's your hot water.'

It was being carried in a wooden tub by a couple of stalwart Indians who slopped it all over the rush matting with cheerful abandon and ducked out again, hands over their

129

mouths.

'Shall I stay and scrub your back?' Patrick asked.

'I can manage perfectly well,' she said haughtily.

'I merely offered.' He spread his hands and went out, half turning as he bent beneath the opening.

The water was hot and scented with pine. The tub was too small for her to do more than crouch in it, but she managed as well as she could, splashing the water all over herself and watching the mud fall away from her bare legs. There was nothing to dry herself on but the blanket. Stepping out of the tub and tipping more water in the process, she wrapped it round her again, trying not to notice the strong smell of stale grease that came from it.

'Are you respectable again?' Patrick asked from outside.

'Yes.' She turned as he came in, feeling an unaccustomed gladness lift her heart as he smiled at her. She had been less than a week in the Settlement but this was the first time she had felt so light of heart.

'Put that on.' He tossed a loose dress towards her.

'Massasoit's squaw gives it to you as a present on condition that she can keep your dress. She's taken an enormous fancy to it.'

'A native dress?' She looked at it doubtfully.

'It's a lot cleaner than yours is at the

130

moment,' he pointed out. 'Shall I turn my back again?'

'You weren't this polite on the ship,' she remarked, turning her own back and wriggling into the garment.

'You weren't a married lady then,' he said, folding his arms and leaning up against the side of the wickiup.

'I'm not a married lady now,' she said, shaking back her hair and trying to tug the dress further below her knees.

'Oh?' He straightened up a trifle, his eyes on her face.

'We're to be married in October.'

'That's more than a month ahead,' Patrick said. 'Scarcely seems worthwhile your coming so soon.'

'Not at all,' she said quickly. 'There is a great deal to do before a wedding, you know.'

'I was never married,' he said.

'Well, there is! the house is not completely furnished yet, and then Peregrine has the harvest to gather, and his own share of the community work to do—' Her voice trailed away as she saw the mocking smile on his face.

'I can see that Master Carver has many heavy responsibilities,' he said.

'Well, so he has!' she said defiantly.

'If I were a marrying man, which I'm not,' he drawled, 'I think I'd be waiting at the harbour side, with the ring in my hand, to grab you the minute you got off the ship!'

131

'Well, you're not a marrying man,' she reminded him, 'so your opinions can't be too important.'

'I always knew that you would turn into a scold,' he remarked. 'Maids with pretty faces often do.'

'Am I pretty?' She raised her eyes to his.

'Sometimes.'

'Only sometimes?' Her face tell a little.

'Sometimes you're beautiful.' He stepped forward, putting his hand beneath her chin, bending to kiss her.

Almost of their own volition her arms wound themselves about his neck and her lips parted under his hard, demanding embrace. For a long moment they were locked together in a timelessness that was like the moments they had clung together in the cabin of the *Bridget*.

Patrick was the first to break away, holding her a little distance from him, the desire in his eyes almost as strong as the anger. She wondered why he should be so angry and then he gave her a small shake, and said.

'I promised myself this wouldn't happen again. I told myself that by now your Master Carver would have whisked you to church to make an honest woman of you, and the best thing for me to do was to stop teasing myself with forbidden fruit. I don't intend to make a fool of myself by wedding anyone and I didn't intend to make a fool of you.'

132

'Isn't it a little late to think of that?' She twisted from his grasp and pushed her fingers through her tangled hair, anger stirring in her. 'Ever since we met, Patrick O'Farrell, you've played with me, now drawing me close, now thrusting me away! It's as if you were trying to punish me for something!'

'Or myself.' He spoke ruefully, the anger gone from his face. 'One day, when you're safely married with a brood of children playing about your skirts I'll tell you a long tale, but not now. Not yet, Mistress Joy-in-the-Lord Jones! Come, we'll go and eat our supper. There's fresh-caught fish and corn bread and I'm hungry.'

'It's very kind,' she said uncertainly, 'but I must start back to the Settlement.'

'Not this evening, I'm afraid.' He stood aside to allow her to pass into the clearing.

'But I can't possibly stay all night,' she began.

'If you imagine that I'm going to tramp eight miles through the middle of the forest in the middle of the night in order to deliver you into Master Carver's loving arms,' Patrick said, 'you are greatly mistaken, mistress.'

'But they will search for me!'

'Not after darkness has fallen if they have any sense. They'll start at first light.'

'Peregrine will be worried to death!'

'A little anxiety will be good for his soul,' Patrick assured her. 'It may even persuade him to pay a little more attention to his betrothed.'

'That's unfair,' she began stormily.

'We'll not argue about it now. Come and eat your supper.' He put his hand on her arm and guided her to where a fire burned. Afterwards she was to remember it as one of the strangest meals she had ever eaten. There were mats set around the blazing fire, and the entire village squatted on them, passing round wooden bowls of a hot stew. There were no spoons. The others either drank the liquid straight down, or picked out the bits of meat with their fingers. The flavour was unusual but not unpleasant. She drank it, enjoying the warmth that began to pervade her. The Indian who crouched at her other side was taller than his companions with a magnificent headdress of feathers and a cloak embroidered all over with shells. There were more shells hanging about his neck and from the pierced lobes of his ears, and he continually smacked his lips after each mouthful.

Patrick, leaning to whisper in her ear, informed her that she had the great honour of being seated next to Massasoit himself.

'And it is an honour. He usually considers it beneath his dignity to sit with a white female.'

'Does he?' Slightly taken aback, Joy turned to smile at the chief who bowed his head with great condescension saying in an unexpectedly musical voice.

'Good food, eh?'

134

'Very good.' She finished the last of it and set down the bowl.

'Squirrel tastes very good at this season,' Patrick said.

'Squirrel!' She gagged a little at the thought of having eaten it.

'Cheer up! The fish is trout,' he comforted. 'In this country the people live off the land in every way.'

'Yes.' She smacked her lips at the chief who responded with another gracious bow.

The trout was handed round on large flat leaves and was picked apart with teeth and fingers. The others who had remained silent, out of courtesy or shyness, began to unbend a little, nodding at her and chattering among themselves in the liquid language that reminded her of water running over stones.

The trout was delicious. Eating it she forgot the taste of squirrel. A large jug of ale was being passed around and several of the men had already drunk more than their share. She moved imperceptibly closer to Patrick and felt his arm slide round her shoulders.

'I told them that you were my woman,' he said, 'so they'll not bother you.'

'*Your* woman! You had no right—.'

'I couldn't tell them you were Master Carver's woman. He would have lost a great deal of face allowing you to wander off by yourself.'

'But *you've* lost face now,' she said weakly.

'Not at all.' He grinned at her in unrepentant fashion. 'I told them I had ordered you to join me and they were duly impressed by your obedience to my authority.'

'Then you took a very great liberty,' she said with as much dignity as she could muster.

'Eat your trout,' he returned unabashed.

'It is good,' she admitted. 'Oh, Patrick, I was so very much afraid! I began to think that I would starve to death, or die of thirst, or run mad with the sun.'

'It's possible but not probable. You were never in much danger.'

'I could have drowned in the marsh!' she said indignantly.

'I'd back you against a bog any day, my darling,' he said, broadening his accent and slanting her a mischievous glance.

She opened her mouth to inform him she was not his darling and then closed it again, mentally shrugging. It mattered little what careless words he employed because they clearly meant nothing to him—as they meant nothing to her, she reminded herself. It was Peregrine Carver whom she had come to wed and whom she loved.

Some of the women had moved out of the circle and were swaying backwards and forwards in time to a thin, high piping that drifted out of the deeper shadows beyond the firelight. Joy's attention was caught by the graceful, sinuous rhythm and imperceptibly her foot began to tap. One of the women came forward, beckoning, and she rose, at first hesitatingly and then, as she was drawn into their midst, with a surging confidence. The melody was sweet and shrill, prettier than anything she had ever heard before. She found herself linking fingers with them as they guided her through the simple steps of a dance that seemed to have no beginning and no end. The steps were easy. The bare feet wove a pattern as they moved back and forth, now facing the men, now stepping aside to change places with one another. The unseen piper sent his tune soaring like birdsong into the sky, powdered now with stars for the sun had long since vanished.

The dance had ended, the last notes dying into the breeze. Joy was no longer with the other women but stood for a moment alone, the music still vibrating along her nerves. Then Patrick uncurled his long legs, and came to her, dark in the starlight. He drew her to him, lifting her, carrying her back to the guest wickiup.

While they had been eating someone had removed the tub of water and laid dry matting over the damp ground. Patrick set her on her feet and looked down at her.

'You were kind to join them,' he said gently. 'It gave them great pleasure.'

'I couldn't have helped myself,' she said simply.

'Dear Joy-in-the-Lord.' He traced the course of her cheek with his forefinger. 'I see

137

you are completely unaware of the meaning of the dance! It's a courtship rite, a way the Algonquin women have of indicating the men who interest them.'

'Then you should not have brought me here,' she said.

'You forget that in their eyes you are already my woman,' he reminded her. 'It would have been a great insult to you if I had ignored such an invitation.'

'I didn't know.' Embarrassment flamed her face.

'And if you had known?'

'I would not have shamed you before your friends,' she said primly.

'If only you were not an honest woman,' he said, shaking his head at her.

Suddenly she wanted to cry out that she was tired of being honest. The storm at sea, the dance in the clearing, both had woken in her feelings that confused and delighted her. They were emotions she dare not confide to him because if she did so she would no longer be an honest woman and something deep within whispered to her that it was her only defence.

'If you will be kind enough to lend me a blanket,' she said, 'I can sleep at the other side of the hut and so not disturb you.'

He stepped away at once, his movements brisk and impersonal as he selected blankets from a pile against the wall. He would not force her or even try to persuade her, she realised. At

138

least he respected her principles, but principles, she thought ruefully, made cold bedfellows.

CHAPTER ELEVEN

It was strange how when one knew the way the landscape immediately seemed less menacing. The darkly sinister woods became sunlit groves and the paths which had been so confusing were now easy to mark and follow.

She had been woken early with cornbread and fruit on which to start the day. Patrick had evidently been up for some time already. She noticed that he was freshly shaved and that he had changed his leather doublet for one of dark cloth. Catching her glance he said cheerfully.

'If I'm to deliver you safely to the Settlement then I may as well appear before them as a respectable gentleman.'

'Are sea captains not respectable then?' she asked, laughing.

'Not if they're Irish and Papist. There are plenty of people in the Settlement who resent having to trade with me at all. Fortunately Governor Bradford is a man of good sense and allows others the freedom of worship he claims for himself.'

'Master Brewster also has been very kind.'

'Brewster is a good man, gentler than many. It means that some people take advantage of him though. You had better borrow my comb if you want to get those tangles out of your hair.'

He had broken off, his eyes on the long strands she was tugging through her fingers.

'That's very kind of you. I wouldn't like Peregrine to see me looking completely disreputable.'

'He should be so relieved to have you back safely that he won't even notice,' Patrick said, handing her the comb.

'Well, of course he will,' she said, 'but it's important we keep up appearances. One must keep up standards even in a savage land.'

'Oh, one must,' he agreed, leaning back and folding his arms. 'One must certainly do that!'

'What are you thinking about?' Dragging the comb through her hair she stared at him suspiciously.

'I was just thinking there's no real need for me to make Master Carver's acquaintance,' he drawled, 'because I only have to listen to you for five minutes to get all his opinions.'

'That,' she said coldly, 'is very rude!'

'I never laid claim to good manners but I give you credit for an independent spirit,' he said.

'Why, so I have!' She shook back her hair and spoke indignantly. 'Didn't I insist on leaving Holland on an earlier ship? And didn't I go for a walk outside the stockade without asking for anyone's permission?'

140

'That showed you're impulsive, without any sense. It doesn't tell me anything about your opinions,' he said infuriatingly.

'My opinions are my own.' She tossed the comb back to him and went out into the clearing. In daylight the village had lost the magic imparted to it by the flaring torches and was a busy place, the wickiups being swept out by the women with birch brooms while copper-skinned, naked babies were tied in wicker cradles and propped up against the outside walls, looking like small parcels with heads on top.

Several men, sharpening arrows and fitting strings of gut to their bows, looked in her direction, promptly covering their mouths with their hands.

'That's their way of showing that you're a respected guest,' Patrick said, joining her. 'When they count you as a friend they'll laugh with you openly.'

'I ought to thank Massasoit,' she began.

'No need. Thanks are only given for extraordinary favours. There is nothing very special about giving food and shelter in their manner of looking at things. If you're ready we'll start out before the sun gets too high.'

'I've no shoes,' she began, and stopped, her mouth opening in surprise. A dusky-skinned young woman had flaunted out of one of the huts, the mud-stiffened skirts of her dress swaying above her ankles, the braids of her hair swinging from a somewhat tattered coif.

'Massasoit's squaw can queen it over the rest of them in that magnificent outfit,' Patrick said. 'She's brought you a pair of her own moccasins to wear.'

'This really is most generous,' Joy said as the girl approached and laid them before her. 'Patrick, will you thank her for me? She'll take thanks, won't she?'

'She's made what she considers to be an excellent bargain,' he assured her, addressing a few words to the girl who promptly went off into a fit of giggling and retreated into her wickiup.

'You speak their language very well,' she marvelled.

'I can just about make myself understood in a half dozen languages. It's useful for trading. Here, let me lace those up for you.'

She had sat down to draw on the shoes of soft leather and he knelt before her, taking her foot in his hand. For a second she sensed it would have been childish to object to what obviously meant nothing to him. He laced up one boot and pushed on the other, flashing a smile at her.

'You and Massasoit's woman have the same size feet. I wager that's about all you have in common though.'

'How can you possibly know that?' she demanded.

'She's got three papooses,' he informed her,

'and from the gleam in Massasoit's eye last night there'll be another in spring. I don't suppose that you can match that?'

'I don't propose to try,' she said, tartly, snatching back her foot so abruptly that he almost toppled over.

'With a temper like that,' he returned, 'I don't suppose Master Carver will get anywhere near you anyway.'

He had walked off before she could reply, leaving her to fume.

Never, she decided, has she ever met anyone who could so easily put her in a dozen contradictory moods in the space of a few minutes! He might say he had no interest in marriage, but she doubted very much if any woman would put up with him for more than a week.

'Are you coming, mistress?' he turned to call. 'I can always go back and tell them you've decided to stay in the Algonquin village!'

'I'm coming!' She ran to catch him up, realising suddenly how much easier it was to run in soft moccasins and a loose, one-piece garment than in tight-waisted dress and buckled shoes.

The path through the marsh was quite clear now that she saw it by day, the emerald of the treacherous ground contrasting with the darker pattern of the firm soil. There were half a dozen of the reddish-brown men accompanying them, their feathers making a brave sight as they leapt from one patch to the next. She envied their agility and grace, feeling incredibly clumsy when they jumped across wide chasms of green where she was forced to hand on to Patrick's hands and be swung over.

The marshy ground behind them, they were soon in the embrace of the woods and again she was struck by the ease with which they covered long distances without apparent haste.

'They never seem to tire!' She sat down abruptly on a fallen log, panting a little as the muscular, near-naked bodies went past her at their steady, unhurried pace.

'They can keep it up for hours,' Patrick said, pausing himself to wipe the sweat from his face. 'They have incredible stamina and they live in tune with the land.'

'You admire them, don't you?' She looked up at him curiously, watching the play of light and shade across his features as the breeze caught the tracery of leaves above his head.

'They're honest and brave,' he said briefly, 'and those are qualities to treasure. They're also illiterate, far too fond of alcohol and full of superstition.'

'You sound,' she said sweetly, 'as if you are describing your own crew.'

'Touché'!' Laughing, he reached for her hand, pulling her to her feet. 'Come, we can walk at our own pace provided we don't lag too far behind.'

'What of your crew? They were not with you

in the village,' she enquired.

'They're on the *Bridget*. We're due to sail in a month.' 'Only a month!' She had not meant to sound so dismayed.

'There's trading to be done and the summer won't last for ever,' he said reasonably.

'Of course not,' she said hastily and drew her hand away.

'Anyway if I stay longer half my men are likely to desert and run off with Indian wives,' he told her.

'Oh, surely not!'

'They make exciting companions,' he said.

She hurried ahead of him, trying not to wonder if he spoke from personal experience. It was, after all, nothing to do with her if he chose to take a native woman to his bed. When she glanced round he was strolling behind her, whistling in a manner that made her quite certain that he had been deliberately teasing her.

They had almost caught up with the other men before he spoke again, 'How is young Mick making out?' he enquired.

'I've not seen him, save at the Prayer Meeting. He didn't look as if he was enjoying it very much,' she confided.

'It will do him the world of good,' he declared. 'In five or six years time Mick will be a pillar of the community with a charming wife and two or three younglings!'

She couldn't help smiling at the picture of

the lanky youth as a respected citizen.

They stopped for a rest at mid-morning, though Joy guessed it was for her sake rather than their own. The Algonquins could clearly have gone on for hours without stopping.

Walking through the woods was so different when one had company. The panic that had assailed her the previous day seemed like a nightmare now. She could look back at it and smile a little at her own foolishness. The Algonquins had slowed their pace and one or two of them risked smiling at her. She smiled back, wishing she could communicate with them in their own language as Patrick did.

They stopped a second time and she recognised the rocks over which water splashed into a pool.

'This was where I got so confused yesterday!' She sat down thankfully and leaned to scoop up water.

'Only a couple of miles to go,' Patrick said, 'I'll send one of the sagamores on ahead so you'll be met with welcoming trumpets!'

'One trumpet would do.' She splashed water into her hot face.

One of the Indians came up and stopped to hand her some dried fish wrapped in a leaf. Patrick was unstopping a leather wine flask and another of the party emptied a handful of tiny wild strawberries into her lap.

'You see you wouldn't have starved even if we hadn't found you.' Patrick smiled at her and she smiled back, her irritation gone as she took pleasure in the joy of the moment. There was a sense of comradeship between them that reminded her of the brief moments they had shared on board the ship. Impulsively she exclaimed.

'Oh, I do wish you were not leaving!'

'I've a living to earn,' he said briefly.

'But you will be returning?'

'One year perhaps. By then you'll be long since wed.'

'Yes.' The thought didn't give her so much pleasure as it formerly had.

'Mistress.' His voice was suddenly sharp and the comradeship had fled. 'Don't marry him unless you are quite certain that you cannot live without him! There is nothing worse than a loveless match. Believe me, but I know it!'

'Know it how?' She fixed her eyes on his face, watching his brows rush together and the line of his jaw harden.

'I was married once,' he said.

'Married! But you said—'

'I said I avoided marriage. That's true. Ours was a handfasting back in Dublin when I was a lad of fifteen. Kathleen was just a year younger and I thought that nobody more beautiful existed on God's earth.'

'Kathleen,' she said slowly.

'She had a small dowry and I'd the promise of an acre of land. That was more than sufficient for our needs. Many marry on less.

However she persuaded me that it would be wiser to keep our marriage secret. We had a simple ceremony—what they call a hedge union, not a church marriage with the priest binding us, but legal according to old law. When I made something of myself then we would tell everybody.'

'What happened?'

'Kathleen went back to her father's house and I went to work on a farm nearby. The farmer had promised me an acre of my own if I pleased him, so I worked! And then I had word from Kathleen to meet her in Dublin. I went, of course, and found her in great distress. An English squire had taken a fancy to make her his wife, she told me, and her father was eager that she should make such a good marriage. I said that we would go at once to her father and tell him that we were already married according to the old law.'

He was speaking as if she were not there, as if he talked to himself, his voice dark with remembering.

'She said that he would likely beat her and I told her I would go alone to see him. We'd met in a little alley and I recall how the moon was just rising above the wall and her hair looked blacker than it did by day. Anyway she agreed that I could speak to her father. He was a mean fellow, Seamus Clare. Mean and grasping! I started off down the alley. I turned to look at Kathleen to tell her not to be afraid. That's all I

148

can remember.'

'What?' Joy looked at him in astonishment.

'I woke up with a thumping headache in the hold of a Spanish ship bound for the Indies. I'd attracted the attention of the privateers, you see.' His voice was light and mocking again. 'It was months before I saw land again and nearly two years before we came back to Ireland. I was older then, older and stronger and wiser than the lad of fifteen who had gone through a hedge wedding with his sweetheart!'

'And Kathleen?' Joy breathed. 'Did you find Kathleen again?'

'I found her.' His smile was not a pleasant one. 'Married to her English squire and living in the grandest house you ever saw. She'd been barefoot when I loved her, but now she'd a pair of silk slippers for every day and gowns with real lace on. I climbed over the wall of her big house and came upon her in the garden.'

'And?'

'I told her that I would take her away with me, that nobody would ever find us and drag us back,' he said heavily. 'She laughed at me. She told me our marriage had never been a legal one, that her husband was a rich man and could give her the fine things I never could. She told me something else too, by way of icing on the cake. Her husband had done business with the Spanish for years. It was he who had arranged for me to be abducted and taken to sea. Kathleen had helped them by luring me to the alley. She told me so quite frankly, laughing as she spoke. She said they could have had me murdered if they chose, but that she hadn't believed I would survive the voyage anyway.'

'You should have killed her,' Joy said tensely.

'I meant to.' He shrugged as if to shift some weight from his shoulders. 'I stood there, looking at her lovely, treacherous face. She wasn't afraid. She believed I was too much in love still to hurt her, but the truth is she wasn't worth the killing. I told myself that one day I would be so rich that I could buy and sell the husband she'd chosen and I climbed back over the wall.'

'The truth is that you still loved her more than you admit,' Joy said.

'Perhaps I've had sufficient time to recover since,' he said dryly.

'And now you are rich.'

'Not as rich as I intend to be. The *Bridget* is my own ship at least and every voyage I take my profits increase. There's nobody who could pay to have me hit over the head and flung into the hold of a ship!' he said vigorously.

'You've not seen her since?' Joy ventured.

'Nor been used and flung aside by any female,' he said. 'Now I am master and owner of the sweetest little ship that ever rode the waves and that's the truest female I ever knew.'

She wanted to cry out that he was wrong to

150

judge all women by one treacherous one, but the words stuck in her throat. She had been on her way to marry Peregrine when she had allowed Patrick to kiss her, and he could scarcely have forgotten that so soon.

'I've not told that tale for years,' he said, 'but you may take it as an apology for the way I teased you and an explanation.'

'For what?' she asked in confusion.

'For not being the sort of man you ought to take seriously, for trying to make a fool of you for my own amusement, for not making you stay with me in that Algonquin village.'

He laughed as he spoke but the hardness was still in his face.

One of the Indians who stood a little way off glanced across at them and then came closer, speaking in his rapid fluent tongue and holding out something in his coppery hand.

'He has a gift for the woman with blue eyes,' Patrick translated. 'It will bring you good fortune.'

It was a little piece of wood, curiously carved and pierced by a leather thong. Patrick took it from the man and hung it about her neck, his fingers touching her lightly and swiftly.

'That was kind of him,' Joy said.

In a curious way the giving of the talisman bound and separated them. His hands on her flesh made her shiver but he had already risen, his voice, brisk to denote, she supposed, that he had regretted the confidence he had made.

'We've wasted sufficient time! Let's be on our way.' She went meekly, torn between the need to prove to him that she was not the kind of woman who would betray the man she had promised to marry and the sudden desire to beg him not to take her back to the Settlement.

CHAPTER TWELVE

They emerged from the shelter of the nut trees into the sloping meadow and she saw the high stockade with its pointed stakes forming a barrier against anyone who might try to get in. Or out? That was a foolish thought because the gates stood wide open until dusk, but she found herself speaking to Patrick low and rapidly as their time together drew to its end.

'You warned me against a loveless marriage, but your own was not and it still ended unhappily. You loved Kathleen and—'

'And she loved money,' he interrupted. 'Anyway she cured me of believing in the good faith of women.'

'Then I will prove you wrong to paint all women in the same colours,' she said tensely. 'I love Peregrine and I will always be faithful to him.'

'Which is why you never protest when I kiss you, I suppose?' he remarked.

That was unforgivable! Joy opened her

mouth to tell him so, but there were people hurrying out of the open gates towards them and Patrick had quickened his step, striding to meet them, raising his voice heartily.

'You see, Mistress Joy-in-the-Lord is safe and sound, and come to no harm at all!'

'My dear, we were so worried about you. God be praised that you are unharmed!'

Master Brewster was the first to reach them, holding her hands between both of his, his kind eyes twinkling with pleasure. 'We sought you yesterday until past dusk and there are men out again this morning.'

'I strayed beyond the fence and got completely lost,' Joy confessed. 'Captain O'Farrell found me.'

'Then we are doubly indebted to you, captain,' Master Brewster turned to shake hands cordially. 'You'll come in and take some refreshment?'

'Thank you, but my friends and I are going hunting, and don't wish to waste the daylight hours,' Patrick said. 'I merely wished to deliver Mistress Jones safely.'

As if I were a parcel or a load of cargo, Joy thought resentfully. She bowed her head coldly, refusing to meet his eyes. She would not allow herself to be drawn close by his charm and then insulted again!

'We are most grateful,' Master Brewster said again. 'Master Carver will join me in that. He was reluctant to cease his search for you.'

153

Others had joined them, exclaiming over the miracle of her return.

'For we thought you torn in pieces or lying at the bottom of a ravine with both legs broken!' Elizabeth said dramatically.

'We searched and searched, but there was no trace of you. It was as if you'd been snatched up by a whirlwind,' Patience Favell added.

'Nothing so dreadful. I merely wandered about for hours wondering how on earth I would ever find my way back again!' Joy said lightly, allowing herself to be marshalled through the open gates. Master Brewster had lingered to talk with Patrick and she didn't look back at them. In explaining his attitude he had confused her feelings more than ever.

'I must find Peregrine. He will be so anxious—or is he still searching?' she enquired, interrupting the flow of chatter.

'He had some work to do in his barn,' Elizabeth said, 'but he was going to search again later.'

'I'll find him.' She set off but turned to ask, as the thought struck her.

'What about Polly? She's been shut up for hours!'

'Mistress Fenton saw to her,' Martha Browne said.

'Thank her for me!' Joy called and, ignoring the tiredness of her feet, set off again at a brisk pace. It was suddenly important for her to be reunited with Peregrine as soon as possible.

154

She hurried up the short path and round the side of the house calling his name, her voice high and eager.

He came out of the barn and stood staring at her, the expression on his face so dark that her headlong rush towards him was checked. She could hear her voice stumbling into an explanation that sounded lame even in her own ears.

'I am so glad to be back again! I was completely lost in the woods and I began to fear nobody would ever find me again! Peregrine?'

Her voice trailed away as she saw his face darken further.

'What on earth are you wearing?' he interrupted.

'Wearing? Oh, Massasoit's wife gave me her dress,' she said vaguely.

'Where are your own garments?' he demanded.

'I fell into a marsh,' she said. 'I was never so frightened in my life!'

'You went to the Algonquin village?'

'Eventually. Captain O'Farrell took—'

'You were with O'Farrell?'

'No, not exactly,' she said swiftly. 'He was the one who found me. I went out to gather nuts.'

'Without leave? It is forbidden for anyone to leave the Settlement alone.'

'The gate was open and I didn't understand

why I shouldn't take a short walk.'

'To pick nuts? Where are they?'

'I ate them,' she confessed. 'I got completely lost as I've just told you!'

'You managed to find your way to the village?' he said.

'I told you that too!' she said, beginning to lose patience. 'I fell into a boggy patch in the marsh and Captain O'Farrell found me. I was covered in mud and Massasoit's wife—'

'Presented you with that indecent garment.' His grey eyes flicked over it. 'Do you realise you're displaying your legs almost to the knee?'

'Is that important, set against the fact that I'm safe?' she said loudly. 'I might have come to some hurt out there.'

'A search party looked for you until dusk, but it was several hours before anyone realised you were missing. I thought you had gone to help Mistress Fenton and she thought that you were with me. They began to search again this morning but in the other direction from the way you evidently took.'

'Then why are you not with them?' she asked bluntly.

'I had the barn to muck out and some corn to get in,' he said. 'The search party returns about midday and I am due to go out in a second party.'

'Then there will be no need for you to bother,' she said testily, 'seeing that to your overwhelming delight I am perfectly safe!'

156

'Of course I am relieved,' he said, 'but you cannot imagine that I am pleased to be regarded as a fool.'

'Who regards you so?' she asked.

'You obviously do,' he returned, 'else you would not have wandered off without telling me nor stayed so long away.'

'Anyone would think I fell into the bog on purpose!'

'Why couldn't O'Farrell have brought you back at once?'

'Because it was almost dark when I fell into the marsh. It was more sensible to spend the night in the village. They were most kind and hospitable.'

'I've not been to the village,' Peregrine said, 'though I believe that Governor Bradford and Master Brewster have been guests there. The Indians performed some kind of dance.'

'Yes, I joined—' She stopped dead, aware that she had already said too much for he was staring at her in undisguised horror.

'You are not going to tell me that you joined in?' he said at last.

'Well, yes, I did. The women were dancing and they invited me to dance with them. There was nothing wrong in that surely?'

'Nothing wrong!' he echoed. 'You must have taken leave of your senses! Nothing wrong to join savages in kicking up your legs— did you wear that garment for the exhibition?'

'Yes, but it wasn't an exhibition!' she

157

snapped.

'Were there others watching this—dance?'

'Well, yes.' She was twisting her fingers together, her eyes beseeching. 'Don't make so much of it! I was lost and covered in mud and terrified.'

'Not so terrified that you did not scruple to wear a most indecent garment and dance for the amusement of others. I presume that Captain O'Farrell was there?'

'Eating his supper. I didn't dance with him if that's what you fear.'

'Perhaps we had better continue this conversation later, when you are more able to listen to reason,' Peregrine said coldly. 'You had better borrow my cloak until you have changed, or did you walk through the streets looking like that?'

'I thought only of letting you know that I was safe,' she said chokingly. 'It never occurred to me that you would be angry.'

'I'm not angry,' he said with an effort. 'I am merely disappointed that you could behave with so little sense of morality!'

'And I am disappointed that you could be so unfeeling as to scold me when I have been in such danger,' Joy retorted.

'I don't mean to scold but you must see how it looks to other people!'

'I don't care what they think,' she said resentfully, ignoring the cloak he held out.

'Nor what I think? Have you no thought for

158

me?' he asked reproachfully.

'Oh, Peregrine, of course I have!' Shamed, she took the cloak and wrapped it about herself. 'I do care very much about your feelings, but I've done nothing wrong! I'm sorry for causing you to fret—it was thoughtless of me to leave the Settlement without telling anybody, but the rest? There was nothing to it at all. Nothing!'

'I don't trust O'Farrell. He's an Irishman and a Papist.'

'I was completely safe with him,' Joy said lightly and quickly. 'I do assure you there was nothing in the least improper!'

'We'll speak of it later,' he said. 'You'd best hurry and change into a decent gown. Cover yourself properly before you cause more scandal!'

'Aren't you going to walk with me?' she asked.

'Later. I'll see you later at the Prayer House.'

'Another prayer meeting!'

'A thanksgiving for your safe return. It might have been a funeral if the Lord had not saved you.'

'It was Captain O'Farrell saved me,' she could not resist saying as she went. 'I doubt if the Lord had anything to do with it!'

She didn't wait for his reply, but walked rapidly back to the front of the house and set off for Mistress Fenton's. It was an interrupted walk. Everybody, it seemed, wanted to assure

159

her of their pleasure in her safe return. Everybody, it seemed, except Peregrine who had been concerned only about her morals. For two pins she would have walked back through the gates and begged Patrick to take her with him; thus giving him excellent grounds for his cynical views about women! She was in a cleft stick from which there was no escape.

Polly flew, squawking loudly, down from the sill of the kitchen window to land on her shoulder as Mistress Fenton appeared at the door.

'My dear, we have been out of our minds with worry,' she expostulated. 'This is not Leyden but a savage land full of hidden perils that a sheltered young girl cannot begin to guess at!'

'I came to no harm.' Joy spoke in what she hoped was a reassuring tone, but the other continued to shake her head and clicked her tongue as she bustled the younger girl up to the tiny loft room.

There was a strange, not altogether pleasant, feeling about stripping off the simple one-piece garment and lacing herself into the tight-waisted, long-skirted gown with its pointed collar. The dress confined her, the skirt hampering her stride, the long sleeves with their narrow cuffs biting into her wrists. She pulled on her woollen stockings and her other pair of buckled shoes and tied her hair back

160

under the little white coif. She had worn such clothes all her life, yet now they felt unfamiliar and strange, and she gave the discarded Indian dress a regretful look before she went down the stairs again.

'Joy, we thought you lost to us for ever!' Sarah Goodright, her flaxen curls bobbing, seized her hands and held them in a moist, affectionate grasp.

'There was no real danger,' Joy was getting rather weary of repeating herself.

'Is it true you spent the night in the Indian village with Captain O'Farrell?' Sarah wanted to know.

'Not really with him,' Joy said, amused. 'He is staying with the Algonquins until the *Bridget* sails.'

'I've never actually spoken to him,' Sarah giggled, 'but he looks very bold and reckless.'

'He's a man your mother would warn you against,' Joy said lightly.

'Is he so?' Sarah flashed her an unexpectedly shrewd look, then chattered on. 'I wished to go out with the search party but Peregrine declared it was no task for a female as we have absolutely no sense of direction.'

'That's the silliest thing I ever heard,' Joy began crossly and stopped, remembering with chagrin that she couldn't present any clear argument against it when she herself had been so woefully confused.

'I have almost finished the cushion covers,'

Sarah informed her. 'They have little ruffles about the edges. They look very pretty.'

'It's been very kind of you to help,' Joy said, wondering how often she would be required to say so.

'I was always rather skilful with my fingers,' Sarah said modestly. 'Peregrine was good enough to say he had never seen smaller stitches.'

'Damn your eyes!' Polly remarked from the back of the chair on which she had alighted. The sentiment was so close to Joy's own thoughts that she wanted to laugh but Sarah exclaimed.

'That dreadful bird! How can you endure to have it near you?'

'Polly's a darling,' Joy said defiantly. 'She understands everything I say and she does everything I tell her to do.'

'The captain gave it to you, didn't he?'

'As a wedding gift.' Joy could not avoid a slight grimace. Patrick had been on the verge of offering her so much more and she dare not accept it.

'When is the wedding to be?' Sarah asked. 'Peregrine spoke of November.'

'October. As I arrived earlier than was planned the ceremony has been brought forward,' Joy said crisply.

'I do hope that I will be able to finish all the sewing in time,' Sarah murmured as Mist ess Fenton came in.

'Now you look like a good Christian maid again!' she exclaimed approvingly. 'We must hurry if we're not to be late at the Prayer Meeting.'

'A thanksgiving for your safe return,' Sarah put in.

'You're not going to bring that bird, my dear?' Mistress Fenton gave Polly a slightly doubtful look.

'Polly cannot endure Prayer meetings!' Joy exclaimed, unable to control her amusement.

'That I can well believe,' Sarah said.

'Polly can sit on the fence,' Joy said. 'She won't fly very far away.'

'Which is a pity,' Sarah murmured, her expression suddenly so spiteful that Joy wondered how she could have thought her pretty.

The bell that called the settlers to prayer was clanging loudly as they walked down the street and people were hurrying to the crossroads where Governor Bradford had already stationed himself at the open door to greet the worshippers. Joy, linked with Mistress Fenton, had a sudden desire to pull free and skip, holding out her skirts and letting her hair blow free. If she did so then they would certainly be shocked at her behaviour. She bit her lip, trying to match her companion's sober gait and modest demeanour.

'Mistress Joy, this is another happy occasion!' Governor Bradford was shaking her hand warmly, his kindly eyes twinkling. 'It is a

163

miracle that no harm came to you but the Lord looks after His own.'

Had she been killed he would doubtless have declared that the Lord took His own unto Himself, Joy reflected, and stifled a sigh. She was beginning to feel as if she was completely out of step in this community of prim and gentle people.

'I fear I caused you a great deal of trouble,' she said aloud.

'We'll not speak of that.' He pressed her hands. 'You are scarcely arrived and are not yet familiar with all our rules. I am sure we can accept Master Carver's promise on your behalf.'

'*His* promise on *my* behalf?' Joy frowned at him.

'As you are betrothed then he will naturally speak for you,' Master Bradford said. 'He has already guaranteed that you will never wander off so recklessly again.'

'Oh.' Her spirits dashed, she shooed Polly to the fence and went inside to the high-raftered hall, no longer feeling the least desire to skip.

CHAPTER THIRTEEN

It was raining. It had rained every day for a week, not the gentle rain that fell briefly at dawns and dusks to refresh parched grass but hard, lashing rain that slanted across the open streets, turning the plots of land into quagmires, soaking through the roofs and the gaps in the wooden walls.

From the window of Mistress Fenton's house Joy looked out at lowering skies and doors stained with patches of damp. Two women, carrying a pail between them, splashed through the mud, holding their skirts above their ankles and bending their heads beneath the rain. Further up the street a small boy, too young to care about the effects of the weather, was jumping in and out of the puddles with great delight.

Joy watched him, wishing that she could capture something of his mood. As a child she had loved to walk in the rain, enjoying the cool splatter of it on her hands and face. Perhaps it was because she was no longer a child, but the weather depressed her. Everything in this place depressed her, she decided, and the sky was growing too dark for her to see the lace on which she was working. It was one of the newly fashioned collars such as she had seen the wealthy merchants' wives wear in Leyden, but such tiny stitches required sunlight. She put the unfinished work aside and rose, smoothing down her skirt. For days she had been confined within doors save for the times when, muffled in a cloak, she hurried to Prayer meeting with the other women. Peregrine had been to see her only once and there had been no time for them to talk very much, Mistress Fenton deeming it advisable to remain within earshot, Peregrine being anxious to return to his work.

'A month—less, and my corn would have been ripe,' he had complained. 'As it is I've managed to save only half my crop and others are in worse case! We'll be on short commons this winter unless the sky clears!'

'If there's anything I can do,' she had begun, but he'd interrupted her impatiently.

'I'm not yet so helpless that I cannot harvest my own grain, Joy! There's a leak in the roof too that will need to be mended. I thought of hiring that apprentice—'

'Mick.'

'Mick, to do it. However it appears it will be at least a week before he, or anyone else, is free to help me, so I shall have to do it myself.'

He had looked and sounded thoroughly out of sorts. Joy had done her best to express sympathy, but the truth was that she felt in need of some herself. Mistress Fenton was kind but her house was small and, as she ran it so efficiently, there was nothing to do but spend long hours reading or sewing or staring out at the driving rain. If she and Peregrine were married, she thought resentfully, at least she would be able to sit in her own house and gaze through her own windows. On impulse she took down her cloak and opened the door. Polly, dozing on the back of a chair, opened one eye and shut it again and from the inner

166

room came the comfortable murmuring of voices. Mistress Fenton's daughter, Susan, was spending the day with her, and the two the them were sharing a gossip over the baking of bread.

It was cold in the street and, if she raised her head, the rain stung her cheeks but the air was fresh and clean and, as she walked swiftly up the street, the exercise made her feel more lively. At the corner as her cloak bellied out in a crosswind she was reminded of the storm at sea and glanced up, to see a darkened sky with roofs beneath instead of mast and sails. She shook her head at her own vagrant thoughts and splashed on down the street towards Peregrine's house. He had spoken of mending the leak in the roof and so would probably be at home. At least she could pretend for a little while that she was already in her own house.

The gate banged to and fro in the wind and the path was filled with puddles. Side-stepping them she went round to the back of the house and put her head in at the door of the barn. The two cows, placidly chewing cud, stared back at her. They at least were warm and dry. It was a good sign in a man when he took care of his animals, she thought, and plodded up to the back door. It was open as she had expected. In the Settlement no doors were locked. There was no bucket set to catch a leak so it must have been mended. She looked round trying to imagine herself as mistress here, kneading

167

bread on the table here in this kitchen, making lace in the swayback chair by the window. The picture remained cloudy, however, as if it had no foundation in reality. Instead she felt a restlessness bubbling up in her that was intensified by the sudden flurry of rain beneath the eaves. She went through into the next room where a small fire burned on the hearth. Peregrine must be somewhere in the house and she opened her mouth to call him, then closed it again.

She had made no particular effort to move quietly. Surely if he were within doors he would have come to greet her by this time. The ladder to the upper storey was too near and too tempting. She had not yet seen the bedrooms and, without further thought, she hitched up her skirt and began to mount.

The ladder—if there were children then it would have to be replaced by a proper staircase—came out in the room directly above. The beds must have been hoisted up through the windows or placed here before the roof was added, she thought, pulling herself up and looking round with interest. Sarah had been industrious. There were already curtains at the windows and a fringed rug on the wooden floor, and one of the beds had a garish red quilt with a pleated border. She walked over to the bed and looked down at it. In less than a month she would lie here in Peregrine's arms. Curiously the thought caused her no flutter of excitement, only a sense of something inevitable drawing near.

There were voices below, Peregrine's tones mingling with a lighter voice.

'Take your cloak off and hang it over the back of the chair. I'll mull some ale to get the cold out of our bones!'

'I can mull the ale.' That was Sarah, sounding eager and faintly breathless.

'You can do most things.' His voice was admiring. 'I don't know how I could possibly have contrived without your help, Sarah. You have gone to such pains to make everything beautiful.'

'It was my pleasure.' Sarah's voice was low. Joy, listening, knew without even seeing them that Sarah was in love with Peregrine. It was only surprising that she had not guessed it before, but it was now so clear that no girl would have gone to such trouble to furnish a house unless she had secretly hoped that one day she might live in it herself. Poor Sarah! How miserable she must have felt when Joy arrived not only safely but ahead of time.

She must have made some sound because Peregrine's voice rose sharply.

'Who's up there?'

She went back to the top of the ladder and climbed down, turning to confront two stiff and disapproving figures.

'Joy, what on earth are you doing here?' Peregrine was the first to exclaim.

169

'I came to—to look round.' It was foolish but she found herself blushing hotly as if she had sneaked in with criminal intent.

'Had you wished to see over the house again then I could have shown you round,' Peregrine said.

'I didn't realise you wouldn't be here.'

'I went to fetch Sarah. She offered to come and do some more of the sewing.'

'As I started the work,' Sarah said, 'I did feel obliged to finish it.'

'Yes, of course.' Joy spoke a trifle too heartily for Peregrine said quickly.

'We neither of us wished to trouble you with sewing already begun.'

'And Joy will be putting the final stitches in her wedding gown,' Sarah added.

The saffron gown with its plunging collar and cuffs of fine lace was ready to be worn but the thought of it gave her no pleasure.

'Sarah and I were about to mull some ale. You'll have some of course?'

'No. No, I ought to be getting back, else Mistress Fenton will think I've gone for another unauthorised walk,' Joy said.

'That incident is surely best forgotten,' Peregrine said. 'It's scarcely a subject for jest.'

'Master Brewster was very lenient,' Sarah put in. 'He could have recommended that the Governor fine you quite heavily.'

'Naturally I too spoke on your behalf,' Peregrine assured her. 'As a coming man in the

Settlement it would scarcely do for me to take a bride who had been fined by the Council.'

He looked and sounded as he always did. Yet it was as if she stared at a stranger across a wide gulf. He was not even a stranger whom she wished to get to know.

'Peregrine will very likely be Governor himself one day,' Sarah said.

'Likely he will.' Joy spoke slowly, her eyes on Peregrine's dull, good-looking face. Dull, she decided, fitted him. Even his coming to this new land had not been the action of a brave adventurer for the Colony had been two years established when he had sailed.

'Will you take some ale?' Sarah enquired.

'From your hands? In the house that is supposed to be mine very soon?' The thought remained unexpressed. Joy said again, pulling up the hood of her cloak, 'I really must hurry back. I see you got your roof mended.'

'Entirely by himself.' There was pride in Sarah's voice. 'There is nothing to which Master Carver cannot turn his hand.'

'Why not go on calling him Peregrine?' Joy suggested sweetly. 'No need to be formal on my account.'

'I'll walk back with you,' he began, but she interrupted him lightly.

'There is no need for you to take another soaking! I can find my way to Mistress Fenton's without hurt.'

'We will see you at Prayer Meeting

171

tomorrow night.' Quite unconsciously he had used the pronoun 'we', thus coupling himself with Sarah. Joy stepped to the door as he opened it and went out, raising her hand in a casual salute, the rain blowing into her face. At least he had the delicacy not to close the door too swiftly, she thought, and felt a ripple of amusement.

She was halfway down the street before she realised that amusement was the last emotion she ought to have been feeling. She should have been filled with hurt or jealousy or *something*. Instead, picturing his shocked expression as she climbed down the ladder and his fumbling attempts at hospitality had made her want to giggle. Yet the mere thought of the unknown Kathleen whose treachery had made Patrick O'Farrell distrust all females rendered her cold with fury.

Joy stopped, heedless of the gusting wind that made it difficult to stand upright, as the truth struck her. 'Struck' was not perhaps quite the right word since this was a truth that had lain at the back of her mind for a considerable period. The only difference was that now she accepted it. She no longer loved Peregrine Carver and she doubted very much if he loved her. The young man who had seemed so dashing to a fourteen-year-old reared in the quietness of the English Community in Leyden now seemed a very commonplace person indeed. Probably Peregrine had suffered the same disillusionment when he had first beheld her trailing up to the gate with Polly on her shoulder, and her unconventional behaviour since must have made him wish most fervently that he had never written to Aunt Hepzibah at all. As for poor Sarah! She must have been deep in love with Peregrine to take such pains over the furnishings of his house. Sarah accepted all the rules of the Settlement without question! It would never enter her pretty blonde head to leave the stockade without permission, or to borrow a squaw's dress, or join in a courtship dance. Sarah Goodright would make a very much more suitable wife for Peregrine Carver than herself, but Peregrine was far too honourable a man to admit it even to himself. He would consider it his duty to marry her and then three people would be miserable unless—

'Mistress Joy-in-the-Lord, what possesses you to risk your death of cold by standing in the freezing rain?' a voice exclaimed.

Master Brewster, muffled in a vast cloak, a broadbrimmed hat pulled low over his eyes, hurried up to her.

'I've been to see Master Carver. He has mended his roof,' she said.

'Peregrine is a most industrious young man,' he approved. 'Certainly he has built up a fine house for both of you to dwell in after the ceremony.'

'Sarah has done a great deal too,' Joy said

fairly.

'She is an excellent young woman. It is the utmost sadness that her betrothed should have died,' he nodded. 'Our first years were difficult. Life is becoming much more civilised now. It is a long and weary business to build a Colony out of a savage wilderness.'

'Yes indeed,' she said dutifully.

'But I keep you philosophising when you ought to be within doors!' He took her arm and began to walk with her, sheltering her from the worst of the wind.

'I believe I have to thank you,' she remembered. 'I would have been fined if you had not spoken to the Governor on my behalf.'

'It is said that ignorance of the law is no excuse,' Master Brewster said, 'but for a pretty newcomer interpretation of the law may be stretched a little. You did cause us all great anxiety.'

'Yes. Yes, I know.' Peregrine had seemed more annoyed than anxious but she let his comments pass.

'And very soon it will be your wedding day.' He gave her a kindly glance. 'Let us pray the Lord sends better weather for the occasion! This is a sad blow to our hopes for the harvest. Still it would never do to question the Will of the Lord. You must not dwell on the misfortunes of our Settlement when you write to Mistress Hepzibah.'

'Write to her?' Joy looked at him in surprise.

174

'Have you not written to her?' He looked down at her, frowning slightly. 'That was remiss of you, my dear. The good lady will be most fearful until she receives word of your safe arrival. If you give the letter to me I will see that Captain O'Farrell is entrusted with it.'

'The captain?'

'He returns to Holland in less than three weeks,' Master Brewster told her. 'He will be carrying quite a packet of correspondence. Next year there will be more brethren coming out to join us. Indeed there is talk of starting a new Settlement some thirty miles north of here. There are some already building and planting there. They are calling it Salem.'

'And Captain O'Farrell will take a letter?'

'For a small fee. One cannot expect him to act as unpaid messenger! You have some money?'

'A little.'

Sufficient to bribe Patrick to take me back to Leyden, she thought rapidly. If I stay here Peregrine and I will be wed as everybody expects, and then we will all be miserable.

'Master Brewster!' Elizabeth Diz was leaning out of the window of her house, waving at him. 'Master Brewster, could you possibly step inside for a moment. My mother is not feeling very well and fancies a prayer might make her feel better.'

'Prayers always makes one feel better any time,' he called back, 'but physic too is often

175

most useful. What ails your mother?'

'A cold, Master Brewster. She has been very hot and shivery.'

'I'll come in at once. You'll be kind enough to excuse me, Mistress Joy?'

'Perhaps I could help,' she suggested. 'My aunt gave me some of her own herbs and showed me how to distill them into remedies.'

'I may very well call upon your services,' he said, and splashed away through the puddles.

Joy continued her interrupted walk, new excitement stirring in her. If Patrick was returning to Leyden then he could take her with him on the *Bridget*. She would have to leave the Settlement secretly but she would be doing the best possible thing. With herself back on the high seas Peregrine would be free to marry Sarah Goodright who would be a much more suitable bride.

'And I', Joy thought, pausing to stamp the mud from her shoes. 'I will have six weeks in which to make that stubborn Irishman realise that not all women are like Kathleen.'

She opened the door and was greeted by a squawk from Polly whose feathers ruffled up as if in welcome. From within Mistress Fenton called.

'Is that you, Master Brewster?'

'He went over to Mistress Diz,' Joy called back. 'She is suffering from a cold.'

'He promised to call this morning.' Mistress Fenton came through, wiping her hands on a

176

small towel. 'Elizabeth's mother is not very sick, I hope?'

'Only in need of prayer.'

'There are one or two others suffering from the cold sickness. 'Tis the sudden change in the weather,' Mistress Fenton said. 'Susan had a bad headache herself so I sent her home. Your own cloak is soaked!'

'Oh, I never catch cold,' Joy said cheerfully, hanging her cloak near the fire. 'On board ship there was the most dreadful storm and I got soaked to the skin but I didn't get a sneeze from it.'

'My dear.' The older woman glanced at her, hesitated, then rushed on. 'It might be better if you did not mention your voyage too often. Oh, you may speak of it to me, of course. I can keep my own counsel. But you did, after all, travel quite unchaperoned and in the company of a Papist—'

'We never discussed religion. Patrick doesn't consider it very important.'

'And that is exactly the kind of remark which can be easily misunderstood! And you ought not to call him by his Christian name. To do so implies a certain—'

'Intimacy,' Joy supplied.

'I was going to say "familiarity",' Mistress Fenton reproved. 'Your having spent the night in the Algonquin village caused some unfavourable comment among the less kindly members of our little Community. It really is not wise to add fuel to the flames.'

'If people really have nothing better to do with their time than gossip then let them,' Joy said flippantly.

'It is very wrong of them,' Mistress Fenton agreed, 'but a young girl must have a care for her reputation. It is not wise even to give the appearance of scandal.'

It was apparently no cause for scandal that a girl should help a man furnish a house in which he and another girl intended to live. Joy was tempted to make a sharp reply, but it was rude to argue with one's hostess, so she said meekly, 'I shall be very careful not to give offence.'

'I'm sure you will.' Apparently at random the other added, 'And Master Carver is always so very correct. He is not a man to be tolerant about mistakes.'

'I'll go up and change my shoes,' Joy said. 'Unless you wish me to fetch Master Brewster?'

'No, he'll be here when his duties permit. There is talk of forming a new choral society,' Mistress Fenton said. 'Several of our young people have complained there is little to occupy them profitably in their leisure moments and I felt the singing of psalms might prove a welcome diversion.'

'Without causing scandal,' Joy agreed and stifled a sigh as she went upstairs.

CHAPTER FOURTEEN

There was to be a special Prayer Meeting, not of Thanksgiving but of Petition. The rain that had lashed the Settlement, ruining the corn and exposing the weak spots of even the sturdiest building, had given way to dull, damp weather, too warm for the time of year, lacking the crisp snap that heralded winter. Every morning Joy woke to a thick, white fog that crept inland from the sea, crawling the muddied streets and blocking out the stockade.

'Half the crops are ruined, my friends,' Governor Bradford said at the Thursday meeting, 'and it will be necessary to ration all supplies this winter until we can plant again. We shall not starve but we shall all grow a trifle leaner in the months to come.'

He had smiled to take the edge from his words, but there had been no answering smiles from those who listened. Famine was an ever-present threat and the chance that no supply ship might call during the harsh winter something to be dreaded.

'What concerns us more is the sickness that has risen in our midst,' he continued. 'We must give thanks to the Lord that the disease has not yet claimed any lives, but a low fever of this type weakens its victims. My own opinion is that it is carried in the warm wind when that wind blows at the wrong season, and as God sends the wind it is to God we must send our petition.'

'God', Joy thought, with a touch of cynicism, could be blamed for practically everything.

'We must turn our minds and hearts to the doing of good,' the Governor proclaimed, 'and thus avert the displeasure of our Creator.'

God, Joy decided, must have an extremely spiteful side to His nature if He sent rain and sickness when He was feeling cross. All about her people were nodding and murmuring 'Amen', but she could not join in. More and more, as the days went by, she felt herself isolated from the Community, no longer in sympathy with their most cherished beliefs.

'An excellent discourse,' Peregrine said as they came out into the drifting fog. 'Governor Bradford always puts the situation so clearly!'

'I must go over to Patience Favell's. She is not well, not at all well,' Mistress Fenton put in. 'I am quite anxious about her.'

'Shall I make up one of the remedies Aunt Hepzibah gave me?' Joy asked.

'No, my dear. I did persuade her to take a dose the other day but she declared it made her feel no better,' Mistress Fenton said, somewhat hastily. 'To tell you the truth I am *most* anxious about her! She shows no improvement whatsoever—indeed I fear that she is growing weaker! She has a dreadful cough and her night sweats leave her completely exhausted.'

She nodded a greeting and farewell to the company in general and plodded off.

'That is a good woman,' Peregrine said, gazing after her. 'Nothing would please me more but that you should model yourself after her.'

'Mistress Fenton is past forty!' Joy exclaimed.

'I doubt if she has altered much since her youth,' Peregrine said. 'It is a great pity she could only ever have the one child. Larger families are far more pleasing to the Lord.'

Joy had a sudden, flashing vision of herself in twenty years' time, the ripeness of her curves blurred into fat, a string of boys and girls, all resembling Peregrine, at her heels. Peregrine himself would be greyer and stiffer and never for one moment would he admit even to himself that he had married the wrong woman.

'Susan is expecting a child in six months' time,' she said. 'Mistress Fenton is pleased about that.'

'She will be delighted when the baby is safely born,' he agreed. 'Are you going to make a gift for the child? Sarah was telling me that she intends to knit a shawl.'

'Sarah told you about the babe already? Yes, I suppose she would.'

'Sarah tells me most things,' he said, looking uncomfortable. 'She and I are close friends,

181

though it is well within the bounds of propriety.'

'I'm sure it is,' Joy said gloomily. He would never, in some reckless moment of passion, seize a girl and kiss her into trembling, and I, Joy thought, would be extremely indignant if he ever did any such thing.

She left him to greet a couple of the men and made her way up the dripping, mist-wreathed streets towards Mistress Fenton's. There was little point in delaying longer. Every day that passed brought the departure of the *Bridget* nearer. Already she had written a letter to Peregrine, crouched over the paper in the privacy of her bedroom.

'My dear Peregrine.
'After much heartsearching I have resolved to return to Leyden. I have great respect and affection for you but none of the deeper feelings which a bride ought to have for her groom. I do beg you to understand and to pardon me.
'Your sincere friend
'Joy.'

It was a stilted, inadequate letter, but the best she could do. No doubt Peregrine would be annoyed, but she was fairly certain that his pride, not his heart, would be wounded and even more certain that deep down he would feel a sense of relief that she was gone. In due

182

course he would realise that Sarah was a far more suitable wife.

She had packed her trunk. It was not large but it was heavy, though she had left behind the remedies that Aunt Hepzibah had supplied, and the quilt. No doubt Mistress Fenton would find some use for it. She would have to carry it the mile to the harbour where the *Bridget* rode at anchor. There was always a boat near the shore with a couple of men fishing from it, and she could ask them to row her out to the ship. The greatest danger lay in the possibility that someone might see her lugging the trunk through the gates of the stockade and Peregrine feel obliged to demand that she stay, but the mist was still heavy in patches and many of the settlers huddled indoors after the Prayer Meeting.

She dared not stay too long else Mistress Fenton would be back. She could wait until evening, she supposed, but the gates were locked at dusk. She would have to take her chances now. She had left the letter for Peregrine on her pillow where it would be quickly found and no doubt, when his first rage was spent, he would recognise her good sense.

She picked up her trunk and carried it, somewhat awkwardly, down the stairs into the living room. It took some moments to coax Polly to her shoulder. The bird disliked the damp and the fog and spent a large part of each day huddled in a corner with feathers drooping

183

and head tucked under her wing. Perhaps she had begun to pine for the captain, Joy thought, and found herself in complete sympathy with the parrot.

The street was deserted save for a small girl swinging on the gate of her home. Joy hesitated, deciding it would be wiser to stop for a word rather than risk suspicion by hurrying away, but the child had spotted her first and, to the other's surprise, jumped down from the gate and ran up the path towards the door of the house. Somewhere further up the street a shutter banged. Joy took a last swift look around. The fog, wreathing about the houses, had an unpleasantly warm, clammy feeling, and her footsteps created muffled echoes behind her as she went on towards the gate. She met nobody else. In one way it was a pity because she would have liked one last glimpse of those who had welcomed her on her arrival but it would have been difficult to explain why she was carrying baggage.

The sparse woodland that stretched between the Settlement and the bay had a path clearly marked. There would be no possibility of getting lost today even though the sea mist was becoming thicker. She plodded on, conscious that the trunk was getting heavier with each step she took. More than once she had to set it down while she straightened her aching back and flexed her fingers.

The long mile was finally accomplished. She

approached the long slope of tussocks and sea-holly that stretched to the curving beach. The mist was a fine white curtain blotting out the seascape and Polly, clinging to her shoulder, gave a dismal squawk. Then it was all around her and the taste of salt was on her lips. She set down the trunk and peered ahead just as a vagrant gust of wind sent the mist spiralling into puffs of cobweb. The sea was as grey as the sky and as empty. Neither boat nor ship rode at anchor near the shore or on the horizon. The possibility that the *Bridget* had already sailed had never occurred to her and for a moment she was numbed by the disappointment. Surely Patrick would not have sailed away without a word!

An instant's reflection convinced her that that was exactly what he would do, by way of making it absolutely clear that he had no serious interest in her. For days she had put off the moment of leaving, fearful lest a too precipitate departure might give Peregrine time to fetch her back, and now that she was here there was no ship. She had made a complete fool of herself!

For a moment she had the strongest inclination to sit down on her trunk and burst into humiliating tears. The moment passed as she reminded herself that she had already given way to impulse once already that day. The most sensible thing to do would be to hurry back, in the hope that her absence would not

185

yet have been noticed, destroy the letter she had left and submit to marrying Peregrine. That prospect made her want to weep all over again but there seemed no other course of action.

Someone was hurrying towards her, zigzagging between the trees. The mist lifted sufficiently for her to recognise Mick, then closed down again as he reached her side.

'Mistress Joy, you were spotted going through the gate!' He was panting and held his hand to his side. 'I ran so fast I gave myself a stitch! They'll all be here in a few minutes, so you must get away afore them!'

'How? I cannot walk on the water!' she said bitterly.

'You must leave your trunk and run into the woods. The sagamores will hide you for they think you're Captain Patrick's woman anyway.'

'Patrick has sailed.'

'Only down the coast aways to load furs. We can find him easy. Hurry else they'll be here to arrest you!'

'Arrest me?' Joy stared at him in bewilderment. 'I'm not a prisoner in the Settlement, you know. If I choose to go instead of wedding Master Carver that's my affair!'

'They're coming to arrest you for devil dealing,' Mick said. 'I heard some of 'em talking after the meeting when Mistress Fenton had gone, saying how everything has

186

gone wrong since you came and how you should be taken up and charged! I ran fast as I could.'

'Devil-dealing! That's the silliest thing I ever heard!' Joy exclaimed. 'You must be mistaken.'

'No. Mistress. The Governor and Master Brewster was trying to calm them down but some of the women were hot against you. And then someone said you'd been seen sneaking through the gates and that was proof positive.'

'Proof of nothing and so I shall tell them!'

'I'll be in trouble for taking your part, mistress,' he said, looking as drawn as his healthy youthfulness would permit. 'They might think I have truck with the devil too.'

'Then don't stay,' she said crossly. 'Here! take Polly with you. I shall go back and tell them how foolish they're being.'

'I do beg——' he began and stopped, frowning slightly, his head tilted. Faintly, through the dank mist, she heard the sound of voices. Mick whistled to Polly who promptly hopped to his shoulder; cast an imploring look towards Joy, and vanished into the curling fog.

The voices were coming closer. She drew a deep breath, picked up her trunk again and started back towards them, her feelings a mixture of indignation and amusement. Mick must have got his tale mixed. Nobody in his senses could possibly believe for one moment that she had dealings with the——

187

'There she is!' Hands reached out of the mist to clutch at her. She struck them away, raising her voice to demand, 'What ails you? I'm here!'

'Running away!' someone called. 'That's clear proof of guilt!'

'Guilt about what? And I'm not running away,' she protested.

'She's carrying a trunk!' Sarah cried accusingly. Out of the circle of faces hers was visibly triumphant.

'We cannot stand here discussing the matter,' another voice put in. 'The maid has a right to be heard.'

'You will have to come back with us.' A man whose name she had not yet learned spoke apologetically, though she saw that he had bent down and was taking a firm grip on her trunk.

'I was on my way back,' she said, but they had pressed in around her, and she had the uncomfortable impression that had she made the slightest protest they would have dragged her back against her will. As it was there was nothing for it but to walk with as much dignity as possible, their voices and footsteps muffled by the fog as it swirled and thickened about them.

The gates loomed up ahead and she was seized in a warm clasp.

'My dear, what made you run off in such a fashion?' Mistress Fenton demanded. 'I cannot, for one moment, believe you guilty of such weakness, but your running away looks so bad.'

'What wickedness am I supposed to have done?' Joy asked loudly.

There was a moment's silence. Then a babble of voices assailed her ears, the women's being loudest and shrillest.

'There was never rain like this until you came!'

'You consort with a Papist!'

'And everybody knows Papists are next door to the devil in their beliefs and practices!'

'Ladies, ladies! Let us be calm!' William Brewster was thrusting his way towards her, his good-natured face full of concern. 'Mistress Joy, there have been charges laid at your door. For my own part I think them to be baseless, but such accusations must be answered else they will fester. If you will come with me to the Meeting House this matter can be quickly cleared up.'

'Not in private where none can hear!' Sarah cried. 'We have the right to question.'

'Was it you who laid the charge?' Joy swung round upon her to say.

'It was my duty,' Sarah began. 'For some time I have suspected—'

'For some time you have looked for a means of getting rid of me so that you can have Peregrine for yourself.'

'That is a foul lie!' Sarah retorted.

'Let us go to the Meeting House,' Master

189

Brewster said wearily. 'You will both have the chance to give your views.'

Joy was being swept along in their wake as helplessly as a cork bobbing on the surface of the sea. It seemed such a short time since she had slipped out, her trunk in her hand, with nothing in her head but the desire to board the *Bridget* and leave Peregrine free for Sarah to wed. Now she was being hustled back as if she were a criminal.

'This is an informal enquiry,' Master Brewster said to her reassuringly, but when she turned automatically towards the women's bench he shook his head and motioned her to a stool set in the corner.

'The repentance stool! I've nothing to repent!' she exclaimed.

'That's not for you to decide,' Sarah said. There was no mistaking the spite in her voice.

Joy threw her a furious look and sat down abruptly. Candles had been lit and burned brightly in the sconces around the walls and a lamp hung over the table at which the Governor was already seated. The other settlers were crowding in. She glimpsed Peregrine who kept his eyes carefully averted from both herself and Sarah, and felt a spasm of contempt for him. He must have known that this was in the wind, yet he had said nothing to warn her, and now he tried to behave as if none of this had anything to do with him.

'Let us begin with a prayer that in this place

190

only truth will be spoken and only justice will be done,' Master Brewster said loudly over the hum of conversation.

There was an instant silence, heads bowing and hands folding in habit. Then a voice called from the back. 'What use is prayer when we have a devil worshipper among us? Let Mistress Goodright put her charges!'

So it had been Sarah who had instigated this! Joy sent her a look that ought to have shrivelled her up, but she stood her ground, her face pale and virtuous.

'This is not a trial,' Master Brewster began.

'Nevertheless the allegations must be heard and answered,' Governor Bradford said. 'Mistress Sarah, place your hand on this Bible and, mindful that it is the Word of the Lord, state your charges.'

'This is stupid', Joy thought. In a moment someone will protest and Sarah will be overruled. But nobody spoke or moved and as Sarah walked to the table, laying her narrow hand flat on the black leather of the immense Bible, she felt the first shiver of real terror.

CHAPTER FIFTEEN

'Now, mistress, say what you have to say,' Governor Bradford said. 'Remember that your hand rests on the Holy Book.'

'Mistress Joy has brought nothing but trouble since she came,' Sarah said. 'She came alone to begin with, in company with a Papist.'

'Captain O'Farrell is a man of honour and his beliefs are his own,' the Governor said.

'But she travelled alone with him against all custom, no other woman being with her!'

'This is not an immorality charge, so the means of her coming is irrelevant,' Master Brewster put in.

'Well, it shows the kind of person she is,' Sarah insisted. 'And she left the Stockade without permission to seek out the captain!'

'I went for a walk to pick nuts,' Joy said.

'Without a basket?'

'I gathered some in my coif!'

'And left your hair unbound which is a shocking thing to do, and came home in a garment that showed all your legs!'

'This is not to the point,' the Governor said wearily.

'She has a familiar spirit,' Sarah said. 'A bird that swears and blasphemes. She boasted to me that the creature will do anything she tells it to do!'

'This is ridiculous,' Joy said, but Sarah was in full flow.

'Since she came the weather has altered. First there was the rain that spoiled much of the harvest and then this mist.'

'We have had mist before!' Mistress Fenton objected.

192

'It never stayed so long before! And the sickness—we have not had a sickness like the one we have now before! She is not sick, is she? She is new to this land and not used to its conditions, but she is not sneezing and shivering, is she?'

'Neither are you!' Joy flared.

Governor Bradford hid a smile with his hand but Sarah was off again, her words tumbling over one another.

'I have had dreams, terrible dreams in which she appeared to me all wreathed in serpents with the devil behind her. I knew it was the devil for he had horns and cloven hoofs and spoke in Latin as the Bible tells us.'

'Actually,' Master Brewster observed, 'the Bible tells us no such thing.'

'She wears something about her neck!' Sarah cried. 'I caught a glimpse of it when she was bending. Those who serve the devil wear his token just as some Christians wear the cross.'

'You seem to know a lot about it—for a good Christian!' Joy interrupted, and surprised another smile out of Governor Bradford.

'And she ran away!' Sarah said in triumph. 'She crept away with her trunk and that's proof of guilt.'

'It's certainly proof of great foolishness,' Master Brewster agreed. 'Why and where did you think you were going?'

'Back to Leyden,' Joy said flatly.

193

'How? You were not expecting to swim the ocean, were you?' the Governor enquired.

'She hoped to be carried in the arms of the devil,' Sarah said.

'I hoped to persuade Captain O'Farrell to take me back to Holland,' Joy said impatiently. 'Peregrine, I'm sorry. I wrote a letter to you and left it on the pillow at Mistress Fenton's house but it's clear that nobody has found it yet. It's a pity that you didn't, Sarah, because there was no need for you to concoct your tale of devil-dealing. I don't wish to wed Peregrine Carver and so I told him.'

'How have I offended?' Peregrine spoke up for the first time, his tone deeply aggrieved. 'What have I done?'

'It's not what you've done. It's what you are! You're a fine model citizen and a sincere Christian, and I would be bored with your company in a week!' Joy said, 'I'm sorry, but you force me to speak plain. I don't love you and you don't love me. If you did you'd never have let another girl make all the furnishings for the house we were going to share! And you'd never have let me be taken up for devil-dealing—you couldn't believe anything so foolish!'

'There have been such doings. People have had truck with the Evil one, and been burned for it.'

'Not here,' Governor Bradford said. 'We have no such burnings here.'

'Ask her what she wears about her neck,' Sarah snapped.

'I suppose you mean this!' She tugged the leather thong over her head and held it out. 'One of the Indians gave it to me. It's supposed to bring good fortune. I took it out of politeness because he meant it as a kindness and then forgot about it.'

'Do you believe that tale?' Sarah asked scornfully.

'I have seen similar ornaments on the Algonquins who come into the Settlement,' Master Brewster said, examining it and then handing it back.

'And the bird? It's against Nature for a bird to talk like a human being!'

'Mistress, there are many aspects of Nature that none of us understand yet,' the Governor said. 'For my own part I see in such marvels proof of the infinite variety of the Creator.'

'And the rain and the sickness?' she persisted.

'The Lord sends them both. No minion of the devil has such powers,' Master Brewster said. 'Your allegations are frivolous, girl.'

Sarah, her face crimson, sat down abruptly.

'As for you, mistress.' Governor Bradford put the tips of his fingers together and gave Joy a long considering look. 'I find no evidence of devil-dealing but your conduct has given rise to very great scandal. From the first you have set yourself against the rules of this community, behaving in a free and easy manner unbecoming in a female. You must tell us now, frankly, if you are prepared to accept our rules of conduct and abide by them.'

'I cannot.' She rose from the stool, holding her head high though her voice shook with nervousness. 'I pray you to try to understand and to excuse me, but I cannot marry Peregrine and I don't want to stay here among you. Oh, it's not your fault but my own! You are all good and kind and I am full of restlessness. I'm sorry, but I don't fit in! I believed that I could, but I cannot! I cannot!'

'Then what is it you want?' Master Brewster asked.

'I want—something more than a stockade and a list of rules,' she said. 'You came here because you were not free in the old world, but you're not free here either! You build too many walls here.'

'There are walls in Leyden too,' the Governor said gently.

'Leyden is not the only place in the world,' Joy said.

'But you must settle somewhere, my dear.' Master Brewster leaned forward. 'If I allow you to leave where will you go?'

'She goes with me,' a voice said from the door. Every head turned as Patrick O'Farrell, his scarlet shirt brilliant against the more restrained garments of the settlers, strode through the congregation. By the door Mick, his expression a patchwork of excitement and apprehension, had firm hold of Polly.

'Captain O'Farrell, I scarcely think—' Master Brewster broke off, darting a helpless look at the Governor.

'I am here to offer Mistress Joy marriage,' Patrick said.

'To a Papist?' Master Brewster looked faintly shocked.

'I'll not interfere with her faith and, as I seldom get the opportunity to practise my own, there should be no difficulties,' Patrick said briskly.

'But where would you live?' the Governor asked. 'You couldn't expect a wife to go back and forth across the seas for the rest of her life!'

'It's time that I settled down,' he said carelessly. 'The *Bridget* would fetch five hundred pounds and with that we could begin.'

'Here? I scarcely think—'

'Not here. Your ways wouldn't suit me at all,' Patrick said, looking amused. 'I would go further down the coast. There's virgin land there and it's rich land. I was reared on a farm back in Ireland and I never lost the love of the land even when I was on the high seas.'

'You couldn't begin a Settlement all by yourself,' Master Brewster objected.

'Those of my crew who don't want to sign on under different masters can take Indian wives and settle too.'

197

'It would be a solution.' Master Brewster looked hopeful.

'I would be willing to give my consent,' Governor Bradford said slowly, 'but the person most concerned is Master Carver. He has built a house for his betrothed and has the right to keep her to her promise.'

'I relinquish that right,' Peregrine said stiffly, and Sarah's face glowed with sudden hope.

'Then it's agreed,' Patrick said.

'Mistress Goodright, are you willing to withdraw your allegations of devil-dealing?' Governor Bradford asked.

'I suppose so.' Sarah's voice was reluctant, but the glow was still in her face.

'I would like a private word with Captain O'Farrell,' Joy began.

'And I with you, mistress.' Patrick took her arm and led her to the door. Behind them Master Brewster's voice was raised above the hum of conversation.

'Let us give thanks to the Lord for such a fortunate outcome to this matter.'

'You don't want to marry me!' In the mist-swirled street Joy shook her arm free of his clasp. 'You don't want to marry any female! You consider us fickle and treacherous and you prize your freedom!'

'Freedom unshared can be a lonely thing,' Patrick said. 'You'd not consent to be my mistress and live with me without benefit of clergy, would you?'

For a moment the vision of Leyden and Aunt Hepzibah flashed before her and then she heard herself say.

'Yes! Yes, I would, if I couldn't have you any other way!'

'And that's why I want to marry you,' he said simply. 'I want you to have everything you deserve and more than you expect! I've known it for weeks, since that night we shared the storm together, but I told myself that you had the right to choose, the right to discover for yourself what you truly wanted. When Mick told me that you'd left the Settlement and then had the courage to go back and face those idiotic charges, then I knew I couldn't let you marry anyone but me. I'm probably the only man on this continent who would put up with you for more than a week anyway!'

'Poor Peregrine,' Joy said and giggled, the strain of the last hours falling away. 'I think Sarah will make him a very suitable wife.'

'A maid of sterling qualities,' he said gravely. 'But what of you, Mistress Joy-in-the-Lord Jones? Will you grow dull and prim when I put a ring on your finger? What kind of wife will you be, my colleen?'

Without hesitation, as the mist lifted in a sudden gust of wind, she pulled off her coif and let her hair blow free.

199

'God damn my eyes!' Polly squawked from Mick's shoulder.

'Exactly!' said Joy and put her arms round the captain's neck.

We hope you have enjoyed this Large Print book. Other Chivers Press or G.K. Hall Large Print books are available at your library or directly from the publishers. For more information about current and forthcoming titles, please call or write, without obligation, to:

Chivers Press Limited
Windsor Bridge Road
Bath BA2 3AX
England
Tel. (01225) 335336

OR

G.K. Hall
P.O. Box 159
Thorndike, Maine 04986
USA
Tel. (800) 223–2336

All our Large Print titles are designed for easy reading, and all our books are made to last.